Author

FESTIM FAMELARTI

04/26/2016

Lost in American Dream

THE FROZEN HEART: YOU CAN MELT IT, OR BREAK IT.
IT ALL DEPENDS ON WHAT'S IN YOUR RIGHT HAND: A
LIGHTER, OR A HAMMER?!

FESTIM FAMELARTI

YOU KNOW THAT I'M SINISTRAL, AND I'M SORRY IF I
THINK RIGHT, BUT I USE MY LEFT HAND...

FESTIM FAMELARTI'S ALTER EGO

Dissolve to:

A conversation with Oscar Wilde.
After I told Oscar that I was writing a book called *Lost in American Dream*, he came close to me and softly whispered in my ear, "If you want to tell people the truth, make them laugh. If you don't, they will shoot you."
I laughed, and then replied, "I think I'm enough of a comedian to make people believe that I'm kidding, if they pull out their guns to shoot me because I told them the truth."
Oscar frowned, because he knew that no matter how witty you are, people will hate you anyway for exposing their flaws. "What I'm afraid of is that people might dislike my book because of the dirty, filthy language I use. I'm afraid they'll misinterpret the metamorphoses! Once a parent told me, "You poisoned me with a book. I should not forgive that. Festim, promise me that you will never lend that book to anyone again. It does harm."

Oscar smiled at me, sarcasm leaking from his mouth, and told me, "My dear brother, you are really beginning to moralize. You will soon be going about like the converted and the revivalists, warning people against all the sins of which you have grown tired. You are much too delightful for that. As for being poisoned by a book? There is no such thing. Art has no influence on action. It annihilates the desire to act. It is superbly sterile. The books that the world call immoral, are the books that show the world its own shame. That is all. But we won't discuss literature."

"I think people are afraid of what's inside them. Blood, Love and the Truth." I said to Oscar.

CUT TO:

INT. MY LIFE – PAST – PRESENT – FUTURE

TODAY IS FRIDAY AFTERNOON

One hundred and six, one hundred and seven, one hundred and eight, one hundred and nine, one hundred and ten. Hooooo! Ab workout done. Now a thirty second break before push-ups for the final time in my room, on the second floor of my childhood home.

My father was a military general. He had twenty soldiers under his command during the war, and not one was wounded or killed. That's good, but it makes me wonder if he was hiding sometimes. Well it's nothing serious, just a thought.

When other members of our big family would come to visit our home, my father always made me play soldier; he gave me orders and I obeyed.
"Stand still. Turn left, turn right. Stand still, relax. Stand still, relax. On your knees. On your stomach. Crawl two meters, five meters. Stand up, relax." said my father, "I'm proud of you, you can go now."
I was just a child, and Franz Kafka felt like an insect, and I was an insect.

He was trying to implant this idea of being a soldier in my head for so many years, but I always loved movies. Even now, I'm preparing for the new role that I'll play in United States of America. Twenty-eight, twenty-nine, thirty. Hooooooo, I exhale.

My father thinks that I'm crazy for wanting to go to America. As a nationalist and a socialist, he always thought this way. His ideas about what makes a country great all revolve around socialism. But being a nationalist means that you have to give up humanism, and without humanism you cannot be a socialist either. So how do we solve this problem?" my father asked.

I answered, "Let's go to America. We will make good money and live good lives. Fuck nationalism."
He cursed at me and screamed, "They are fascists."
And Franz Kafka would love me for my courage.

I go back on the ground for another set of push-ups. One, two, three... thirty. I stand up and exhale, hoooo.
Also my father added, "They are worse than..." I walked outside and shut the door behind me. I didn't hear him finish his sentence, but I guess that he was trying to tell me that in America you have no freedom. But I know for sure that there is freedom, and with good will and hard work you can be anything you want to be.

Back to the ground for my last set of push-ups... twenty-nine, thirty. I lift myself up onto my knees and exhale, and I wonder how my father can think that there is no freedom in America when I've watched American television and, for the first time, seen a pussy on TV. I mean, how much more free can you be? You can flash your reproductive organ on television.

Anyway, I never paid too much attention to my father's speeches, especially after the war. To be honest, now that we are living in democracy no one gives a fuck what my father has to say.

I stand up and walk to the pull-up bar that's set up in my doorway. I jump up, grab onto it, and start my pull-ups. One, two, three... twenty. I'm on the ground and I exhale, hoooo...

Now, because no one in our family would listen to him, my father was feeling low, disrespected, unloved, and unwanted by both our family and the people of our country. As much of a motherfucker as my general father is, he found a solution for his problem. The general, my father, that motherfucker bought a dog. A dog doesn't judge your character. You can be anybody: communist, fascist, religious, pedophile... anything, anything, anything... cactus. If you feed him, he will be nice to you and listen to you and he will pretend to love you. He will nuzzle you because he knows that you will give him food and he will survive for another day.

…Eighteen, nineteen, twenty. I'm on the ground and I exhale, and my father, since he bought his dog for the purpose of self-soothing, is feeling younger and more powerful. Someone is still listening to him when he gives orders. Self-soothing is very important. You have to find the method that is good for you, but be sure not to tell anyone that its purpose is comfort. If you do, then people will know that you are weak. You'll have no power over others, and this means no respect for you. You'll be unloved, unwanted, heading straight into the abyss. Oblivion.

One final set of pull-ups. One, two, three... twenty... back on the ground, gasping for air.

Yes, my father has a dog, a little puppy. He doesn't love or even like him, but he is the only living thing that the general has power over. He could tell the dog to lick his balls, and he would do it, because a dog is such a fucking loser that it listens to anything. My father never told him to do that, though, because he doesn't like losers licking their balls. He keeps convincing himself that he has the greatest puppy ever.

Self-soothing is very important.

After I finish my workout, it's time to repeat the five new English words that I learned today:

1. Self-soothing 2. Oblivion 3. Enormous 4. Significant 5. Lobbyist

This is what I've prescribed myself in order to learn a new language. Every day, I learn five new words. I repeat them ten times during the day and at the end of the day I create a sentence using those words.

I am in the shower, and I jerk off while thinking about God's masterpiece, Marilyn Monroe. In my head I come on her face, and then I wonder how many people every day come on the face of the masterpiece of God. I try to compare this number with the number of people that die every year from mosquito bites (two and a half million), and I justify God with the fact that he is busy making other masterpieces in order to soothe the rest of the world so they can think clearer and be happy.

Thank God, because of his masterpiece I was able to decide to live the "American Dream". Tomorrow I leave town via car to the border of Italy, and from there I will sail by boat to Spain. In Spain I will take a freighter through the Atlantic Ocean and I will be in Mexico in less than two weeks. In Mexico I will meet a man, and via good boots made in Italy, I will cross the American-Mexican border alongside ten Mexicans. In only two weeks I will be in the UNITED STATES OF AMERICA; a step closer to living my dream.

I come out of the shower and I look at myself in the mirror, eight perfect abdominal muscles; chest, shoulders, trapezius, biceps, triceps, quadriceps, gluteus maximus, calves, and thighs, all perfect. I take a towel and I dry myself off while thinking about playing in a Hollywood blockbuster. I wonder how the fuck they could refuse this guy.

You can say whatever you like but without the masterpiece of God, I wouldn't have a clear idea for my life.

By the way, I have a question. Who is your superhero?
Mine is Superman. He can crack your skull with his pinky, he can pierce through your skull with his red laser eyes and blow your head off like a real grenade. He can fly faster than any drone ever made.
Please subscribe below and leave comments.
Peace out.

Before I go to sleep, I have to write the sentence of the day using my five new words.

SENTENCE OF THE DAY: "A **lobbyist** is waiting in the corridor, lost in **oblivion**, thinking how **enormously significant** it would be if he could convince the border to vote for the newest regulation that helps workers with daily **self-soothing**."

CUT TO:

EXT. ON THE OTHER SIDE OF THE WORLD.

Today is the day. On the American-Mexican border, three of the Mexicans that were crossing the border with me are now shot dead. How embarrassing. When people die trying to live a better life, they should be rewarded. They told me that even more people will die there in the future. This eased my mind. They are not the only people murdered on the border. Dying alone is painful, but they are not alone. Being dead doesn't mean no shit if you are alone or in a clique.

Oh fuck. That sentence is not what I meant to say.

I finally stepped into the United States of America, and I must tell you the year in which all this shit is taking place. This is 2015, and no matter how hard it is to cross the border, it's worth every damn hardship.

Next year, another psychotic oligarch has the chance to become president of the United States of America, thanks to the victims who dissolved and change and became ignorant, racist citizens, and who are raped by big corporations and can't help themselves. By choosing another psychotic, stupid fuck, they think they will be un-raped, and that they will make Great White America again. It's worth it to cross the border because doesn't matter who wins the next president-oligarch is going to build a wall and divide people, because that's the only way and oligarch can give orders and rules.

Have you ever thought about all of the times in the history of humanity that politicians are the ones who build walls and separate people, and that the people are the ones who destroy those walls later, after they've been built by those schmucks? Or, have you ever thought about how, all of the times in the history of humanity, the people are the ones who build bridges to exchange ideas and look forward to a bright future, and the politicians are the ones who end up destroying those bridges? I guess you never thought about it. Well, now you have the chance to think.

An hour ago, I saw a video of George Carlin, and I'm wondering what George would make of this situation? I bet he would say, "you people are full of shit, dumb as a motherfucker… . Oh, you people are scum bags."

My cousin that lives in Brooklyn came to Florida to pick me up. We are traveling in a Mustang toward Brooklyn. We don't speak much.

In my first week in America, in New York, I saw all of Manhattan and Brooklyn. It was just as beautiful as what I'd seen on television. In Manhattan, I first saw big buildings reaching for the clouds in the sky. Later, I took the subway. It was crowded, noisy, and kind of dirty, but cool, because it made me feel like I was in the Ninja Turtles movie.

The first place that I visited was Times Square. Oh my God. So many people. So many lights. So many stores. People walking left and right, up and down, not knowing where they were heading. Their dogs were following them. How sweet is that? Ahhhhhh! I've officially begun living the American Dream.
I continue my journey through Manhattan and everywhere is the same: people walking, tourists taking pictures, people everywhere, busy, busy, and busy. A few tears drop from my eyes, and I feel sad for all of the time that I spent in that shit-hole. Fuck. God, I hate my father. All of those years. I will never forgive him. I hope he dies a miserable death, in loneliness and in pain and poverty. I wash off my tears, I smile, and new tears fall from my eyes. These tears are happy tears. I made it.

All the selfies that I took in all those beautiful places, I posted on Facebook, and people from back home were going crazy over them. I had so many likes, and so many comments. I felt important. Somewhere deep inside I knew I wasn't important, but I fought back my sub-consciousness and kept convincing myself that those likes and comments were real and now I still feel important.

I'm in Brooklyn and in almost every store I step in people salute me with PRIVET, KAK TI BE, and KA DELLA. I don't speak Russian. I may be blonde, but I don't look Russian. I think to myself where the fuck are the white Americans that I have seen on TV? I haven't seen them in Manhattan either.

I started working construction with some Russian guys, but I wasn't making good money and I wasn't happy at all. Fuck, I never worked construction even back in Albania. There it's considered a disgraceful, disgusting job, but here I fucking did it. The truth is that I used to cut trees with my father's chainsaw when I was a young boy. He said we would use the wood for fire, or to be more realistic, to warm up his balls, but when we brought down communism I gave up on cutting wood and told my father, "If you want to warm up your balls, you can cut the wood yourself".
And for this, Franz Kafka would go crazy just to have a selfie with me.
The Russian guys I worked construction with helped me get a social security number. It was fake, but it worked. I wasn't happy with the money I was making there so I began to look for a way out. I wanted a shortcut to reach my American Dream.

In order to be considered a specific type of individual, there are certain things you must do to fit the mold. I began to fit myself into the "American" mold, and my first step was becoming a Starbucks member. To be a good American, you drink Starbucks.

I was waiting in line at Starbucks when a man came inside and started screaming: "You people are crazy, you are wasting your time and your money trying to buy some shitty coffee! You're all fucking addicted to worthless stupid shit." And I was about to tell this guy off, when the guy in front of me walked out of the line, grabbed his shoulder, and told him, "Listen you fucking dickhead, we all know that, but get the fuck out of here." And all other people told him yeah get the fuck out of here.

It's my turn to give my order. The cashier asks me what I want, and I tell her I want a caramel macchiato, extra caramel, and she writes this on the cup and then asks me for my name. I tell her JOHN.

Words of the day:
1. Border
2. Mexican
3. Invader
4. Starbucks
5. Hola

Sentence of the day: "A **Mexican invader** who crossed the **border** illegally, walked into **Starbucks** and the cashier greeted him, "Hola, buenos dias señor."

-SPRING-

Now, you can picture me, John, the handsome blonde guy with a perfect body and great ambition; a fucking immigrant. Well, I'm just an immigrant and I'm having this dream: I'm having sex with this American girl, she's loving me and my accent, and I have a joint in my mouth. I'm smoking it and doing her doggy style, and she's moaning and speaking in a sexy way that you hear only in American porn, not from your wife when you do it with her, "yeah baby, harder, harder, spank me, yeah, oh I love it…" She is saying all this as I puff the smoke out of my mouth, and from the smoke my dream dissolves into an Indian place, and slowly the smoke fades away. I see an old native Mexican with fire on his hands. He's blowing smoke from the fire at my face trying to baptize me. I guess he recognized my talent for fucking, so he added the word fucking, in front of the word immigrant, "You are a fucking invader immigrant" and kept blowing the smoke into my face. My dream then dissolved into nothing, and I woke up. I woke up and that's a good thing; enough with dreams, let's be real.

I'm in America now, it's time to work and not dream anymore. As I was saying, I needed to find a shortcut to reach my American dream, and one way to do that was to make faster money. So just like that, I met another illegal invader who was born in Albania too. You have to know one thing about trying to take shortcuts in America. You don't fuck with the corporate world. You have to wake the fuck up, or they will fuck you right, left and up & down. Capiche?

So let me give you a heads up and clear your hopes for my story. If you thing that this is going to be some cool gangster, mafia, drug-selling shortcut, it won't be. Those gangster stories are long dead and gone. You can find them only in movies, and TV shows. The people you see on social media playing gangster and shit; they love to feel like that, but they aren't really. Anyone who wants to be a gangster will end up getting stepped on by the big corporate world. Or how the real gangster would say, 'You would be waked.' *They* are the real mafia. They do all of this kind of business legally: drugs, prostitution, gambling, etc.

My shortcut.

My friend told me that in Washington, even though I'm an invader and don't have any status, as long as I have a social security number I can get a driver's license and a CDL. If I do that, then in a year I can make $100,000, and that is good fucking money for anyone, not just invaders.

Without a penny in my pocket, I planned my life, I'll drive a truck for one or two years, find a girl to marry me so I can get a Green Card, go to film making school, divorce my wife because that's normal here in the United States of America, and do my first film. Boom, faster than the blink of an eye I'll become rich and famous; American Dream Mission Completed. I imagine Sean Penn saying, "And the Oscar goes to the Fucking Invader", and everyone in the theatre is clapping and cheering for me.
How sweet is that?

And I think about different people's reactions when I tell them about my dream to become a filmmaker. One guy said, "Movies? Great, what kind of movies? Porn?! Hahaha, Good luck buddy, don't forget me when you become somebody". Then the next guy, "They are waiting for you in Hollywood, you're gonna make good porn. You're handsome, and they like blue eyes. Don't forget me."

Then my lady friend, "You're gonna make some porn. I know, you idiot, don't forget me. I can give you a blowjob if you want…", and, of course, she got what she wanted, even though I wasn't rich or famous, she did it because she thought I was sweet. My uncle: "Porn… porn, who cares? You know Rocky? He started with porn, and now he's a millionaire. People can talk shit about you, but everyone would love to be in your place. Don't forget your uncle." I'm calculating how badly these people need to be fucked. They need to be fucked really good if they ever want to be something, because if you've been fucked enough then the first thing on your mind wouldn't be fucking. It would be to get a glass of water because you're thirsty and tired from fucking, right?

Words of the day:
1. Alter-ego
2. Antagonist
3.   Scumbag
4. Self-Confidence
5. Escape

Sentence of the day: "When your **alter-ego** is the **antagonist** in the movie you love, or the **scumbag** that you have met once on the road, then you have problems with your **self-confidence**, and you need to **escape** from the people that surrender to you."

Back to business, enough with the fucking, but not with the sex-love story.
My invader friend found me a house in Washington to stay in. He said that I could stay at a Romanian's house, his name is Levin. My invader friend picked me up from Brooklyn with his truck, and we drove for five days from Brooklyn, NY, to Seattle, WA.

Spoiler alert: All invaders have problems with directions, when we try to tell you in which way we, or you, have to go in English. Be aware, to figure out for yourself which way is the right direction. I know you can understand me, you are all Americans.

During these five days of driving, I learned a lot about life. I can compare life to a highway. You're driving on the highway and you think that the car in front of you will drive fast so you follow him. He is actually slow as shit (correction – slow as a slug, shit doesn't move). You thought wrong, and you can't wait for him. You now must pass him. The next person in front of you is driving fast, and you are tailgating. He hits the break hard and you hit him. Big mistake because the accident is your fault. Lesson learned: do not stay on someone's ass, keep distance to avoid disaster. Be independent, don't wait for the others, maybe they are texting someone, or... mmm I forgot the other lessons, but I promise I will tell you as soon as I remember.

My friend Raktim uses Las Vegas for self-soothing. I heard him say Vegas is sexy, cheap and beautiful. He promised me that he would show me best places in Vegas for self-soothing when I start truck-driving. Why Vegas? As a truck driver you are on the road 24/7 with no time to chase chicks.

It's been quite a few pages and nothing big has happened, or maybe we missed the small details? Some simple truths slid under the shadow of the big dream… but remember: simplicity is the other extreme of a matter.

Have you ever thought about that? Simplicity and Complexity, they are both two extremes, and that is why when something sounds simple, it cannot actually be that simple for your mind, because you got used to living in the golden mean.

Funny, huh?

SECOND SEASON THREE 3
-AUTUMN ACHTUNG-

We arrived at Levin's house at almost midnight. Raktim calls him on the phone to tell him that we're waiting in front of his house. We had waited outside for ten minutes when the front door opened, and I was happy, for some reason, because a fifty-something year old white man appeared from behind the door, and I finally felt like I was meeting someone normal.

He walked toward us, and I stretched out my arm to shake his hand, which I guess wasn't his thing, but I insisted on shaking hands and so he gave me his hand. I wished I hadn't insisted, though, after Raktim began a conversation with him.

"You remember when you left Tim?" asked Levin, (Tim is short for Raktim), and Raktim has no idea what he's thinking of, until he added, "You remember, you had to work one more day on the roof, but you left, because you had to start truck driving, and you told me that when you get your first paycheck you would pay for two guys to do the work for me. Something like two hundred dollars?"
Now I know who the fuck I'm dealing with. This asshole is rich. He has eight fucking houses, and yet he's asking for money that Tim didn't even owe him.

I almost spit on his shoes.

Tim wants to finish business with Levin, so he tells him that he'll pay $500.00 for me to stay in his house, $300.00 to get me a car, and $200.00 to pay the workers that Levin couldn't pay for himself. He gave him $500.00 for now and will give the rest after I get the car from Levin.

I hug Raktim, and he hugs me back. We say good night, and he walks to his truck as I walk into Levin's House.

INT. LEVIN'S HOUSE – MIDNIGHT
One big house

The front door opens from right to left. On the left side, the wall is around 4 meters. Then there's a narrow hallway to the left that leads to the two bedrooms and a bathroom.

When you walk in the front door there are stairs that lead to the second floor. At the top of the stairs there is a door, and on the left side of the stairs is a tiny corridor where the sofa that I would be sleeping on is located.

We go back downstairs and from the front door the kitchen area looks like a bus. Further inside, to the right of the kitchen is a living room with a TV. To the right of the living room is a corridor that leads to three rooms and a bathroom.

When you open the front door, on the right side is another living room without a TV. If you are sitting on the sofa that's in front of the kitchen you can see the stairs, the kitchen, and the dining room, like three divided sections.

Do you get it? No? Okay I'll draw it for you.

Drawing of first floor

Drawing of second floor.

A picture is worth a thousand directions.
"GPS"

I look at the house and I allow Levin to lead me to where I'll be sleeping. Of course, he takes me to the second floor and in that tiny corridor there is only one sofa, a small desk, and the American flag on the wall. I wasn't satisfied, but I had to take what I could get. I needed to take my CDL (Commercial Driving License) so I could leave this shit hole.

Levin left, and I was all by myself in this big house. I couldn't understand why he wouldn't give me one of the many empty bedrooms in the house to stay in. Why do I have to sleep in this tiny fucking corridor that is reminiscent of something in a horror movie. I said, "Horror movies, fuck them, I'm going to sleep. I need to think of something else… something like Marilyn Monroe."

I close my eyes and reality slowly dissolves into a dream where I'm having a good time with a few girls, and here and there I sometimes see a blonde woman that looks similar to the one I always dream of when I'm awake. I'm enjoying this dream, until someone comes and tries to cut everyone in half with a chainsaw just as it's about to be my turn.

CUT TO:

INT. TINY CORRIDOR – MORNING
I open my eyes and it's already morning. I look at my phone and there are some notifications. I see that Raktim texted me, asking if I liked the house, but I didn't feel like replying to anyone that morning. I look at myself in the camera, and I fix my hair and take a couple of selfies. After that, I get up. It was already 7:00 AM, and I needed to go to the DMV (Department of Motor Vehicles) to deal with some paperwork, and then I had to start school for my CDL.

I open my bag and I fish out a towel and a new pair of underwear. I put the towel over my shoulder, and I walk downstairs. I turn to the right where two bedrooms and the bathroom are located, and I walk through a narrow corridor to arrive at the bathroom door. I open the bathroom door and HOLY SHIT. I close my eyes and turn around.

An old lady around eighty-five years old is sitting on the toilet seat, naked.

I close the bathroom door, because the old lady is not going to, and I breathe deeply and shake my head, not knowing what to do next. After about ten seconds, the bathroom door opens and the old lady comes outside naked and walks across the hall into a room, and then, from this room comes a huge black man wearing nurse's clothes. He looks to be in his thirties. He turns to the old lady and tells her, in a strong Nigerian accent, "Breakfast is ready, Mona!", and he looks at me, salutes me and walks back to where he came from.

I walked inside the bathroom and locked the door.

My cameraman is still outside shooting this creepy corridor, and I didn't tell him to cut, because I wanted to know what went on inside the house while I wasn't there.
After twenty seconds, out of the bedroom comes the old lady, and she's now wearing a t-shirt and a skirt. She walks through the corridor and my cameraman follows her. She makes a right turn and is now in the living room. Then she walks toward the dining table, and my cameraman meets another surprise.

There are five old women sitting at the table, including the old lady that we just met. I guess her name was Mona, right?

My cameraman keeps recording the situation and it's pretty boring. Nothing happens for five minutes. The ladies were all just staring at each other, sometimes slowly changing the direction of eyesight. They were having lunch. Each woman had a tray in front of them, and each tray held a bowl of soup, a piece of bread, a glass of water, and their pills.

After quite a few minutes, the nurse shows up with another tray in his hand. He walks toward the dining table, places the tray in front of the last old lady at the table, and then goes back into the kitchen. Rosa looks at the food, but doesn't touch it. She stares over at the plate in front of Veronica.
Veronica, another white lady around seventy, was eating her soup very slowly. She needs 45 seconds for each spoon of soup.

On the right side of Mona is Vera, then in the center, on the right side of Veronica, is Shelly
Vera is a black woman around 70 years old.
Rosa is a Hispanic woman, around 40 years old, who is mentally ill.
Shelly is a white woman around 70 years old.
After a minute and a half Azobo comes back to the dining table and looks to see who is eating, and who is not.

Azobo is the nurse from Nigeria. He lives in this house, and takes care of these old ladies. He also seems to be slightly mentally ill, but I'm not sure.

As Azobo looks at the women, he speaks to Shelly loudly, but not screaming, "You finished your food? Aaaa Shelly? Very good.", and walks around the table and stops behind her.

Shelly turns her head, looks at Azobo and smiles, but doesn't say a word. Azobo looks at the small cup with pills and says, "You didn't take your pills?" Now he continues loudly again, but not screaming, "Why Shelly, why? This will help you." He takes the small cup with three pills and brings it close to Shelly's nose and says, "Why you don't take your pills? Look at them. They keep you alive!"

Immediately, Rosa interrupts in a heavy Spanish accent, "Maybe she no want to live", and she laughs a kind of horrific laugh that makes you wish you had never heard it.

Azobo looks at Rosa, who's still cackling, and then opens Shelly's mouth with his right hand, and with his left hand forces the pills into her mouth. Then he grabs the glass of water that was in front of her, and gives her the water, saying, "Good, now drink the water. Very good." He closes her mouth, and helps her swallow the water and the pills by holding her mouth closed.

Rosa is still laughing.

Azobo can't stand her laugh, and asks her again, "Why are you laughing Rosa?", to which she replies, "Because Mona still no have eat, and she too lazy".

Azobo looks at Mona and says to her, "Why you don't eat? You want to die like Shelly. I don't let you die, just let me know why don't you eat?" He walks close to her, and asks the same god damn question again: "Why you don't eat? You want to die like Shelly? No, no, no dying. You are strong woman".
Mona barely answers, "I don't have a spoon".

Rosa is still laughing as Azobo looks at Mona, bewildered. He walks into the kitchen, grabs a plastic spoon, and, as he re-enters the room, Rosa stops laughing, as though someone finally found her off-button. Azobo puts the spoon on Mona's tray, saying, "Eat. You have to take your pills also." Mona does as he says, takes the spoon, and slowly eats her soup.

Azobo moves around the table, and picks up Rosa and Shelly's trays to bring them back to the kitchen. For five minutes nothing happens. Our cameraman starts moving slowly around the dining-room table. Rosa could be seen staring at Mona, as she slowly eats her soup. Shelly silently stares out the window behind Rosa, as Veronica watches Shelly, and Vera holds a book in her hands, staring at one of the pages.

Our cameraman circles around the ladies once and then goes back to his original position. After a minute and a half, Azobo comes back to the dining-room table, and takes Vera and Veronica's trays back to the kitchen, and then tells Mona, "Let me know when you finish, and don't forget to take your pills."
None of the old ladies say a word. Azobo walks upstairs, and for another ten minutes nothing more happens, until Vera gets up and slowly walks toward her room, which is to the right of the dining table.

Cut to me:

I have my towel around my body as I walk into the kitchen toward the fridge. I remove the milk, close the fridge door, and then open one of the shelves to find a glass. I pour the milk into the glass, and put the milk carton back in the fridge. I take the glass in my hand, and I started drinking it while walking out toward the dining table, and guess what? In front of me were all of the old ladies. I step back, and Rosa smiles at me and salutes me, "Hola". I don't reply. I leave the glass in the kitchen and run upstairs thinking to myself that this is a concentration camp for old retired people.

As quickly as I can, I put on my clothes, and run outside as my cameraman follows. After running through the front door, I leave it open so the cameraman can follow behind me, but he instead stops in front of the door, shooting the empty street. After five minutes Rosa comes to the front door, and stares outside while thinking about the fact that the door is now open and that she can run away. But where would she go? So she laughs at her thoughts and closes the front door. She walks slowly to the dining-room table, looks back at the mirror, and then from the mirror turns back and walks to the dining-room table… and so she started her marathon: from the dining room table to the mirror.

For ten minutes Rosa is in first place, she's unbeatable, and she is on her way to break the Olympic record. Azobo walks down the stairs, goes to the dining room table, and our cameraman takes the position where we can see the three sections, the stairs, the kitchen and the table.
Azobo leans his left hand over the table, and, with his right hand, takes the small cup of pills, looks at them and asks Mona, "Mona did you eat? Did you take your pills?"

Azobo saw that she did not take her pills, so he does the same thing that he did to Shelly. With his left hand he grabs Mona's head from behind, and, with his right hand, he opens her mouth and shoves the pills and water inside her mouth, "Great Mona, great. You are my lady, and you finished your food. Excellent."

He takes Mona's tray and sends it back to the kitchen. Meanwhile, Rosa is still doing her laps, and the audience is going crazy for her, "GO ROSA, GO!", and as Azobo is walking back to clean the dining-room table, he grazes Rosa's shoulder. Rosa stops her marathon and stares at him.

After a few seconds Rosa says to Azobo, "Why you hit me?"
Azobo doesn't reply, so Rosa asks him again, "Why you hit me?"
Azobo gives her a quick look and continues cleaning. Rosa screams
this time, "Why you hit me? I'm talking to you Azobo!"
Azobo replies, "What did I do?"
Rosa answers, "You hit me."
"I didn't hit you."
"You hit me."
"Rosa, why are you doing this to me? I'm taking care of you."
"Why you hit me, are you crazy? Do not ever touch me."
"I swear to Jesus, I didn't touch you", replied Azobo while
chuckling and shaking his head.
"You smiling. Why you playing with me? Don't ever touch me."
Azobo stopped cleaning and points his index finger at her.
"Are you crazy?"
"Don't call me crazy, I'm not crazy."
"Rosa, you are not crazy, ok, but why do you think I hit you?"
"You hit me, I'm not crazy."
"Rosa now is day, why are you dreaming during the day? People
dream at night."
"I'm not dreaming."
"People dream during the night, you dreaming now, dreaming
during the day, no stars now Rosa."
"Don't talk to me ever again."
"Okay, I'm not talking to you, but I didn't hit you."
"I'm not listening to you."
Rosa ends the conversation and continues with her marathon from
the mirror to the dining room table. No one knows how many laps
are left until she makes it to the finish line.

Azobo shakes his head and continues to clean the table.

CUT TO:

INT. MY LESSONS

Remember how I told you I was going to teach you a few small
lessons I learned from my experience on the road with my friend

Raktim? Well, once, as we were having an exceptionally interesting conversation, we forgot that we were driving and we missed the exit that we needed to take.

What now?

As the GPS was rerouting we had to drive without knowing where we were going. When it finally gave us a new route, there were an extra fifteen minutes added to the time it would take to make it to our destination.

Sometimes when you miss your exit, you only have to go a mile or so more to take the next exit that will easily allow you to make the U-turn under or over the bridge and head back toward the exit you missed so you can get back on your expected route.

Sometimes when you miss your exit, you have to go a few miles ahead and take an exit that will force you to drive on backroads with sharp twists and turns, which, for a truck driver, is never good news. You have to be careful driving on the local routes with such large cargo in tow.

Sometimes when you miss your exit, you have to drive several extra miles, and take the third or fourth exit out of your way and do the U-turn under or over the bridge, or wait for the green lights to come on, and then drive back, and when you think you've made it back to your exit, you actually can't take that exit from this side of the highway, so you have to keep on driving to the next exit, where you can get off and get back on the other side of the highway to get back on route.

And because I'm in America, and I don't have any time to lose or to add on to my destination, I have to concentrate on my goals, and work smart and hard. So when I saw the old women in the house, and something didn't look quite right to me, I called my friend Raktim to figure out what the hell was going on. Maybe he knew something but forgot to tell me about it.

The phone rang in my ear, until I heard Raktim's voice, "Hello?"

"Hello, how are you doing?", I replied.

"I'm good, just driving."

"Good, good. Hey, I just wanted to tell you that today when I woke up, I ran into some crazy old ladies in the house. They were having breakfast, and, to be honest, I was scared."

"So?"

"So, I just thought it was going to be a little bit nicer than this."

"What were you expecting? A five star hotel?"

"Oh, no, no! Just, you know, I kind of have a fear of old people."

"Well, my friend, welcome to America. You have to overcome your fears to get what you want, or let your fears take over and they will get only what they want." And he hung up on me.

I stared at the phone, thinking about what he said. "He made me think", I thought to myself, "…that's something. Not too many people make me think."

CUT TO:

EXT. LEVIN'S HOUSE – EVENING 9 p.m.

I walk down the street thinking about how my day passed by so quickly without doing anything productive. Once I make it to the front door, through the blurred glass at the side of the door, I can see someone walking to and from the mirror. I knock on the door, and wait for someone to open it. The person that had been walking around inside had disappeared. In a few minutes, the door opened and Rosa appeared, smiling.

"Hola!"

I smiled, and said "Hi. I'm Festim."

And as soon as I said my name, all of the ladies peeked their heads out to stare at me. My cameraman took a close up of my face, and then zoomed back and here I am, in Starbucks giving my order to the cashier.

"Caramel macchiato, please."

"Sure. What size?"

And in my head popped a stupid thought, that size matters, and I answered, "Medium."

She responded, "Grande."

I replied "No, Medium."
She explained to me that grande is actually a medium, and I asked, "If medium is grande then what is small?"
She said, "Small is large."
Once again I get lost in my thoughts and I think this sounds pretty awesome. If some girl asks me, "What's your size?" I can tell her Grande, because I think my size is about medium. She'll think that this guy has a huge cock, and she'll give me the green light. And even better for guys with small penises. Here we go boys, your dick is no longer small, but is actually large! And, believe it or not, I had all of these thoughts in less than two seconds, right before she asked me if I wanted the caramel macchiato, hot or iced, and, of course, I wanted it hot.
Then she asked me for my name, "And your name please?"
"Festim."
"Metstim?"
And the other cashier, "Deststin?"
And another cashier, "Festis?"
And another, "Justin?"
And another, "Fucker?"
And the last cashier, "Can you spell it for me please?", trying to be polite.
"D-J-A…." I had a thought like I was the nigger on the horse in Quentin Tarantino's film, Django Unchained.
"F-E-S-T-I-M"
"Ah. That's a cool name, you have."
"Thank you."
"$5.07, please."
And I gave her my debit card and she swiped it through the machine, gave me back my card, and said, "Thank you, you can wait at the front please."

I go to the front and as I wait for my caramel macchiato, I want to take this time to explain to you why this big misunderstanding happened. It's because of me and the way my accent sucks in such a spectacular way. To be honest, I could practice my accent and probably speak very fluent English, but, welcome to the evolution of language. Language is not only a way of communication, it's also an art, and because modern people are calling everything that is deformed, shapeless, and ugly, modern art, I may as well be the living masterpiece of the twenty-first century.

That's why this book is lost in time and space, it shows the real face of the people who try to speak English. We have a difficult time with present, past, and future tense. That's why this book is sometimes in third person, sometimes in first person, sometimes in past and sometimes in future. But, most of all, this is all just one big dream and dreams are confusing, but you are all, or you will be, Americans, so you're smart and can figure out what I'm talking about, right? And you can't say, "I still don't understand, because that's stupid", I'm speaking futuristic English here, for god's sake. I need an agent to put me up for auction, and I mean to sell me to a big corporation as a piece of art, not as a slave.

"Caramel macchiato, with extra caramel, for Festim", said the barista.
"Thank you, sweetie", I told her.

I grabbed the cup and took a sip, and it sucked, and to be a nice American most of the time you have to swallow it the way it is. When I glanced down at my name on the cup I saw N instead of M: FESTIN. God fuck. And my cameraman takes a close up of me again, zooms out, and we are back in Seattle, in Levin's house.

"Come in", said Rosa, holding the door open for me.
"Thank you."
"My pleasure."

I walked upstairs and got ready to go to bed, hoping, first, that I'll wake up again. Any one of these crazy old women could wake up in the middle of the night and cut my throat, or piss on me, or do some other crazy shit. And second, that I don't have nightmares. Fuck, I have a lot of nightmares, but there's only one thing that makes me face my nightmares, and that's my goal, my dream.

I remember what my communist father once said: "If you have nightmares, that's alright son. This means that you are also having big dreams, and only when a dream is too big can you get lost in it, and the result, until you find your way out, is your nightmare. That's the beauty of it: finding yourself when and where no one else can find you."

And I know my father was right, even though he was a communist. I know that if he knew about technology, he would say, "Son, those people who were completely lost, guess what? I found them scrolling with their index fingers, up and down, on their smart phone screens." And I know that he would say this is just for the fuck, but also to show me how fucked up their lives are, and wonder how I could want to become like them, and then he would fart and laugh at the end of his sentence.

Fucking communist.

Anyway, I'm going to sleep now.

Words of the day:
1. Festim – Celebration
2. Small
3. Close-up
4. Find

SENTENCE OF THE DAY:
"As the cameraman is taking close-ups of the people in this small celebration, I find myself staring at the beautiful lady smoking a cigar."

INT. NIGHTMARES - DAY

The nightmares you have during the day can be scarier than those you have at night.

You can see the whole nightmare, as well as all of the closed gates. Your hope is gone and even from the very beginning you tell yourself that you're done.

In nightmares that happen at night, you cannot see anything. When that happens, you begin to believe in and create things that never existed in the first place. Your hopes become greater, and in the end you can die more easily: a faster, and less painful death.

Oh fuck. Fuck. Fuck. I'm back in my country, and I don't have any money. A fucking immigration officer busted me and sent me back home. Fuck. I have nothing. Why did I go back? This is not possible, I'm surrounded by mosques and churches, coffees, chairs and dogs that are trying to eat me. I'm running; trying to find a way back to America.

Why?

I just don't understand. Why is it that my worst nightmare is to be back home? Home is supposed to represent safety, happiness, and love… not the opposite.

It's bad, really bad, and I know that every immigrant's worst nightmare is to go back home. Work hard, because your real home is where your job is done, not where you were born. Where you were born means nothing. Free yourself from nationalism, from religion, and corrupt corporations. Your home is the entire galaxy.

Everything is losing its meaning. Home has become a nightmare.

While I'm still at home I remember the time immediately after war, when everyone came running to invest in this tiny wounded part of the world. Corrupt corporations, Muslims, Christians, Chinese, private people from around the world… except the Jews, of course. They only invest in their holy land. Fuck the others. We are the chosen ones.

When I say everyone came to invest, what I mean is that they came to take a greater part for themselves, while they invest their time on us.

Corporations corrupt politicians, so that they can make our country a big McDump. Muslims and Christians, build their temples so they can convert as many poor and desperate people who come from the war, and maybe later to fight for god, of course.

Chinese people built their own little stores selling everything for a dollar, everyone would shop there, and that's how much it costs to have a life back in Kosovo after the war. This cheap price was awesome for all investors, you could buy a genius for a dollar, you could buy an engineer for a dollar, a doctor's price was going for 0.69 cents believe me or not, and don't make me talk about artists and athletes. Two artists you could buy with 0.10 cents, and the same for one athlete. You had to be tough to escape from this disaster.

The money that was given for education, was stolen by the investors.

After all of this, let me give you one page of peace.

All of you who are reading this book, you may say that the story of the place where I was born has nothing to do with my big dream, and I lost my exit, but you are wrong. This is the exact exit I was looking for you. Just think about it, if you want to get rich quick, start a war. On the backs of the wounded people, and through the ashes of murdered people, you can build your corporate empire. It always works.

Now I'm in the middle of a football field, and Marilyn Monroe is jerking me off with her right hand and with her left hand she's playing with my balls. She's good with both hands, and as she's giving me a hand job, she is looking at me with her beautiful blue eyes. She's licking the head of my dick, and I dive into her blue ocean, completely lost, happy, and proud of myself for what I've achieved in my dreams. And yeah, yeah, ohhhh, I'm about to come, and I'm loving it, but in a dream, right before you come, your consciousness wakes up and you're aware that you're in a dream, and you start to feel embarrassed that you'll come on your bed, as well as in your dream… but if Marilyn is giving you a blow job, fuck consciousness. You insist to continue your dream and this is the greatest brain war between sub consciousness and consciousness. If co your consciousness wins, you wake up and you feel like shit, even though you just came. In my case right now, my dream won. I didn't wake up. So I'm coming, and Marilyn was not the kind of girl who would let you come in her mouth. She recognized that I was about to come so she tries to move her head back, but I put my hand behind her head, over that beautiful golden hair of hers, and I hold her head and come in her mouth. Yeahhh. She starts choking in a way, and ouch, she hurt me, fuck. I pull out my dick from her mouth and it's hard to see if there are any bruises when your dick is completely covered in spit and sperm, but I keep looking at my dick. I think that there are no bruises; the pain is coming from inside.

Marilyn disappears, my dream dissolves, and I'm somewhere else, but the pain in my penis is still present and I can't control myself. I have to piss almost everywhere. As a young man, I cannot stay home. I have to walk in the city, wandering around, chasing girls, and even though I know that, after two minutes I have to piss somewhere, and just like that, for almost a week, I pissed in every mosque, in every church, in every temples, in every office, in every coffee, and, I have to tell you, I almost pissed myself.

Once, as I was pissing in front of a church, I glanced at a sign in front of me that said, "Church of Jesus Christ – Private property, violators will be persecuted".

And right there, a man or a woman dressed completely in black with a sword in his/her hand ran after me and I woke up.

CUT TO:

INT. LEVIN'S HOUSE – MORNING

I'm a morning person, I wake up early and I don't sleep well.

Nightmares.

Again and again. Night after night.

I woke up this morning at 6:00 A.M.
After a short sleep and a long nightmare, I felt kind of dizzy, stressed, and depressed… like I would after a night of drinking.

Hungover.

You know, when you're hungover, if you drink more alcohol you'll feel better, so I thought that maybe sleeping was similar. If I slept for another hour after having nightmares I thought I'd feel better. So I quickly check my phone and I see a few Facebook notifications… nothing important, a few people liked an old photo, three "friends" invited me to join their fan pages, five people have birthdays today, two girls poked me, and twenty friends sent me invitations to play games, but no one texted me to ask me how I'm doing, and no one liked or commented on a status I wrote the other day regarding government birth control and the brainwashing of children around the world by religious parties, nationalist parties and corporations. Eh, I guess that isn't their thing.

My father would say, "Most people are completely lost", and that if I want to get a few likes I have to post a photo of my abs.

Oh, my abs!
Since coming to the U.S.A., I hadn't had the chance to do any exercise.
I'm beginning to lose my fit shape. Well, at least I can justify it. I've been busy since the moment I arrived here. I haven't had time to do anything, really.
My time is flying by in America, and I don't really know what's happened.
Is it the money?
Or is it my American dream?
Or am I dissolving into something else? Am I going to be broken in the blink of an eye?
These questions have been on my mind for a while.
You know what, I'll just get up and start exercising. I can do push-ups, a bicep workout, triceps, trapezius, abs, I can do every workout I possibly can just to remain real.

I get up and begin by stretching and running in one place to warm up my body.
This is, to exercise, how foreplay is to sex. It usually doesn't take very long, though.

Some people say, "I'm going to work out", some say, "I'm going to the gym", some exercise, some work on their fitness goals, some do bodywork, some do this and some say that. I prefer the word exercise; to me, it just sounds so much more serious than the other phrases and words. Then again, it's just me and I may be wrong, but who knows.

After I warm up my body in complete silence, trying not to wake up my 'roommates', I start my exercises, beginning with push-ups. One, two, three… twenty. Hoooo… I exhale and I'm happy that after that long pause I can still do twenty push-ups in one set. My father is still a communist, and my father would say to you, "You scrollers, keep scrolling", and nice asses are still one of the most talked about topics in media.

Jesus, some things never dissolve into anything else, the only way to convert their energy into something new is to break them up.

Oh, did I tell you that my father bought a dog? Yes? And that he uses him for self-soothing? Yeah? He named him Stali after the worst dictator of all time, the evil psychopath, Stalin. It's funny though, hearing my father calling his dog, "Stali, Stali, Stali, Stali, come to papa! Look what I've got for you!" It is so sweet to see my father playing with his dog that, if you didn't know him, you would give him five yellow stars for his behavior, but just as you did, he would refuse your reward. He'd spit out all of your yellow stars, and would ask for only one red star.

I lay back on the ground and start my second set of push-ups: one, two, three... twenty. I exhale again and again. When I think about my father's dog, I feel sad. He's a victim of my father. He was named after a mass murderer, he stays with my communist father all for a piece of bone, just because my father changed his strategy and decided he's into caressing and pretending he loves animals.

My father's dog will never evolve and rise up to have human level intelligence. He will never be rational, and therefore he is a victim of my father. When my father was a general he killed dogs, and they never had a chance to see their lives in a different way, now that he's taking care of his dog, he is fooling him with entertainment in the form of throwing tennis balls back and forth through the house, and keeping his dog busy with this game and with that game, with caressing, and with his bone.

Too much hurting and too much taming may be antonyms, but they are both synonyms for the word 'busy'.

All species of animals are victims of human intelligence.
They will never evolve or have the opportunity to grow and obtain a human level of intelligence, as long as we continue killing them, torturing them, or taking care of them. What they need is to be free. They can take care of themselves.

Oh, I forgot to mention something! The corporate world is the human race, and me and you? We are the animals.
Like it or not, most of us look like horses.
Hardworking, loyal, trustful people. Ready to give our souls to the fields for our masters.
Oh, poor good people.
It's simple this way. THINK: the human race is a king, all of the other animals are the king's subjects. Have you ever heard of a king who gave his throne to his subjects?

I get back on the ground and start a new set of push-ups. One, two, three, four… twenty. I exhale, and inhale, and I exhale and inhale, and I exhale again, and I hear someone on the first floor, and I think to myself that I must have woken up one of the ladies. I didn't mean to.

My mother was a wonderful lady, the queen of the kingdom, and I feel sad for her too, she was a victim of the system and a victim of my father, too.
I carry her pain on my shoulders. I always tried to help her.
She wanted me to become a doctor.
How sweet is that?
She had a great heart, bigger than the whole world, and, of course, she thought of me. She wished that I would be a great doctor, that I would help people and take care of them, just as she did for me and my brothers and sisters.
I miss her so much. Every time I think of her, I cannot hold in my tears and so they flow from my eyes. As a pure liquid, my tears touch my heart and dissolve it into some kind of spiritual, miracle spell, and make me feel grateful for everything around me.

I get back on the ground again, and do another set of push-ups.
One, two, three… twenty. Hoo… I exhale.

My father and my mother had that kind of love, they were ready to die for one another.
And my father always said that only two communists could love each other unconditionally.

Looking at their 45 yearlong marriage, I guess he was right. They never fought, they only had small, insignificant arguments, and it was always that one of them had started it. If my father would start to complain, the topic would be about the country or the people, and if my mother started complaining, the epic would be that we needed a new dishwasher, a new vacuum, a new oven, a new this and a new that, the children needed better clothes.

She was a wonderful woman, and she wasn't even a communist. I know that deep inside she was a democrat, she loved democracy, and you know what's funny? My mother had a poster of Marilyn Monroe, and she used to keep it locked in her closet, and no one knew about that poster except for me and my mother.
For my mother, Marilyn Monroe represented a beautiful, free, open-minded woman. For me she was a first love, and my dream. Here and there, I would open my mother's closet, take the poster of Marilyn, and stare at her for a couple of seconds. I'd hypnotize myself until some outside noise would bring me back to reality, and I'd put the poster back where it came from and walk away.

I begin my ab workout, one, two, three… twenty. I exhale, spread my arms, and I lay on the ground. As I'm staring at the ceiling, the facade is showing me figures of different things that were lost somewhere deep in my subconscious, and I try to connect the dots on the ceiling. I try to figure out those images to give sense to the ceiling. And I create the list of Lost and Found things, and one of them was my love, not Marilyn, I mean my real love, Sofi.
Sofi, the most beautiful, charming, delightfully alluring, classiest woman of all time.
Every man and every woman fell in love at first sight. She was hard to get, and you had to be patient. You had to show her that you're worth it, otherwise you would only ever be like me: dreaming about her.
Oh, and forget about conquering her heart with force.
The heart of a lady like Sofi, you can't even think of giving the slightest push by force.
You can only win her over with love.

Most of the people who fell in love with her, gave up on chasing after her, but they'll forever remain in love with her and will always keep dreaming of her. Even when they make love with their loved one, they will think of her.

Sofi, the essential matter of life.

I continue my ab workout. One, two, three… twenty. Hoooo…. I exhale again and I lay again on the ground and I start connecting other dots on the ceiling, and my list of Lost and Found is on two long papyrus pages.

The left papyrus page, and the right papyrus page.

On the left page are the lost things, and on the right page are found things. Of course, my right papyrus page is much shorter than the left page. If I unfold the right page, I'm not proud of myself at all, and I'm embarrassed to tell you that if I unfold the left papyrus page I could wrap it around not only the earth, but also the sun, the moon, and even other galaxies.

If you are lost right now, and you don't have any idea what's going on, just keep moving. I promise you will find yourself on the right papyrus page in the end.

I continue my last set of abs and when I finish, I exhale and again lay on the ground and try to connect different dots on the ceiling, and this time nothing makes sense, everything is lost, and for a second I think I'm going crazy. I'm trying to connect dots on the ceiling and give them meaning. The other day I was talking to God, and the first sign of craziness is talking to things that doesn't exist. God-Man. What's going on with me? I'm losing my mind; I must pull myself together before I fall completely apart.

I feel my muscles burning, getting stronger and dissolving into the masculine strong man form they were always meant to be. I take a selfie, and this eased the pain in my mind, called deep thinking.

A good selfie always helps me increase my self-confidence, and likes on Facebook are responsible for releasing the hormones of happiness, endorphins, dopamine, serotonin, in my body.

'Science has discovered that likes are as equally profitable as masturbation for the human body and mind.' -Dr. Festim Famelarti

The way to respect one another has changed from actually helping one another to simply giving likes to one another.
How sweetly the world is dissolving into the sun.
I'm loving it.
After posting the selfie of me smiling with my eight perfect abs, right away I received a few likes. This is progress, and I stop my exercise and give people some time to like my new selfie. I pick up my towel and some clean underwear to go take a shower in the bathroom downstairs.

As I'm walking downstairs, I meet Azobo. He was already awake, and in that moment I had a few thoughts about this house.

When I met the old ladies for the first time, I hoped that there might be a beautiful nurse taking care of them, and believe me or not, my insane, sexy thoughts started creating the best porn movie you have ever seen. The type of porn with nurses riding hard cock. But goddamn, as soon as my eyes caught the big Nigerian man in front of me, my sexy thoughts cut to a prison cell where little white boys were being ass-raped by big black men.
By the way, why does it always have to be that white boys get fucked in their asses by big black men?
Is it the size of a black guy, or is it the sweet ass of a white boy?
Why isn't anyone afraid of Chines prisoners? Maybe their issue is their size, but their speed could cause destruction in the blink of an eye. Before you'd even know it, they would have already finished three times and when you'd look at yourself in the mirror you would see the cum of three different Chines men on your face like sour milk.
The whole world is a big lie, it's all propaganda.
Be careful out there when you see Chines people. It will be far too late when you look at yourself in the mirror.

I walked inside the restroom, undressed, and began to take a shower, and no matter how sexy I am, you don't want to see me soothing myself.

My cameraman, of course, understands and he walks toward the living room and goes in its place where he can shoot the three sections, the stairs, the kitchen, and the dining room table.

INT. BORING SCENE

Azobo was preparing breakfast for the sweet old ladies.
Each tray contained a bowl of chicken soup, but without pieces of chicken meat, two rolls of bread, a plastic knife, a small plate of raspberry jam, a tiny cup containing three pills, and a glass of water.
Azobo, carrying two trays as he walks out of the kitchen towards the dining room table, says "How are my ladies this morning?" with a big smile on his face. He stops at the dining room table between the chairs where Mona and Vera are sitting.

He served those two trays to Mona and Vera, then he went back to the kitchen and took two more trays to serve to Veronica and Rosa. The last two trays taken from the kitchen were for Shelly and for himself.
He took a chair and sat.
Hold on! His meal tray was different than that of the ladies.
The food looked better and he had no pills to take.

Azobo stretched his hands to reach out to Shelly and Mona, so he could start with a prayer before they began eating.
Shelly hid her hands, and Mona doesn't move hers from the table.
Azobo closes his eyes and starts praying out loud, "Dear Jesus, thank you for this beautiful morning..." the ladies began eating as soon as he closed his eyes.
In the same time, in the bathroom I was masturbating and I was so close to coming, and Azobo continues, "...thank you for this food, thank you for our health, help our ladies to live long and healthy. In the name of the father, the son, and the holy spirit. Amen."
I just came, and ohhhhhh... I open my eyes, and in the exact same second Azobo finishes his prayer and opens his eyes.

Azobo starts eating his food, and as he eats he doesn't even glance at the old ladies.

Once he finished his breakfast, he raises his head and sees that Shelly didn't eat at all.

"Why, Shelly, you not eating?" asked Azobo, and Shelly didn't show a single sign of life.

Azobo continued, "Eat, eat, or Mona will take your food.", and right after Azobo finished his sentence, Veronica farted so loud that everyone could hear it.

Azobo looked at her and shook his head, as Veronica tilted hear head and slowly got up out of the chair and began walking toward the restroom.

"Where are you going? Sit, sit, and finish your food first, then I'll take you to the restroom. Do you have your diaper on?", asked Azobo.

Veronica nodded.

"Good, sit now, and finish your food" said Azobo, and Veronica did as he commanded.

Azobo sniffed like a dog a few times, and he couldn't handle the smell.

"Veronica my dear, I think it is better if I change your diaper now. Please get up again, and walk with me to the restroom."

Veronica got up and followed Azobo.

Azobo prepared the toilet and a fresh diaper, as Veronica slowly walked inside the restroom.

Azobo closed the door, and after two minutes Veronica opened the door of the restroom and walked naked into the hallway.

"Where are you going? Come back! You don't have your diaper on yet.", said Azobo and Veronica stopped and looked towards the dining table, pointed at it and said, "But…"

"But, come back first and put on your diaper"

This is Azobo's job. Taking care of retarded, old people.

CUT TO:

EXT. FRONT DOOR – LEVIN'S HOUSE

It's my third day in Levin's house, and Levin still has not given me
the car as he promised, and I have not given him all of the money
yet.

After a nice morning, and some self-soothing in the shower, I come
out of the bathroom, go to my 'room' on the second floor, change
and get ready to leave the house.
As I open the front door, I see that it's pouring rain outside, nothing
to wonder at, as Washington is a very rainy place.
As I was staring at the wet street, Levin came down the road with
his old, almost broken down car. He stopped the car in front of his
house, walked out, said good morning to me, and walked inside.
As he walked inside I thought to ask him to give me a ride to the
CDL school, or at least to the bus station.
I turned my head back and was ready to walk inside to ask him, but
I see him coming back my way, so I stop him.

"Hey Levin, how are you this morning?"
"Good, you?"
"Good, Levin, could you give me a ride, please?"
"Where to? Not too far?"
"I guess not… to the closest bus stop."
"Ok, hurry up, get in the car.", said Levin, and I got inside the car
and Levin started driving.
As he's driving, I ask Levin, "Could you give me one of your cars,
as you promised, and I'll give you the money?"
"Money, oh yeah, don't forget about that"
"What about the car, I need to go to school."
"What car?"
"The one that we made the deal about."
"Oh yeah, of course, the car. You have to be patient."
"What do you mean, I have to be patient?"
"Jesus was patient, he taught us patience."
"Patient? I won't be here for too long, so I need the car as soon as
possible"
"Oh boy, patience. You have to be patient and things will come to
you, this is what Jesus taught us. Things will never come to you as

you want." He finished his statement, chuckled and looked at me with his evil face.

"Well, Levin, I'm an atheist, I believe in you and me, I believe in our deal."

"Oh, so you are an atheist?"

"Yes, I am."

"No good, no good, this is very bad. Let me tell you what happens when you die."

"When I die?!"

I wished I could dissolve into a computer virus and create chaos.

"I had a few ladies like you that I took care of, and when they died their faces were sad, and desperate, and their skin turned into a white-yellow color, and they had smelly, disgusting bodies…"

I thought that was what happens to everyone when they die, but no, Levin had more to say,

"… and the Christian ladies when they died in my arms, you should see their faces. They were smiling, and light shone from their faces, and they were happy because they knew they were going to a better place."

Levin was almost finished with his speech, and in my head I thought that any place is better than Levin's shit-hole house. I had to stop his speech, so I told him, "Don't put Jesus between our deal. I need the car. Stop blaspheming."

"Stop blasph… what?"

"Nothing, just find me the car."

I thought how people seem to know more about each other more than they understand about themselves, and I'm not wondering anymore when I hear them speaking on *your* behalf. Be strong, God, and accept the truth that your people know shit about you that you wouldn't like to be heard from the whole world.

We arrived at the bus station and he stopped his car. I walked outside wondering how those people who speak on behalf of God really don't know the meaning of the word blasphemy.
I guess I'm still wondering after all.

Words of the day:

1. Diaper
2. Abs
3. Negro
4. Picture
5. Nailed

Sentence of the day:
The picture of a black Jesus nailed on the wall shows his
magnificent negro abs, and the white diaper portrays the pure soul
of Christ himself.

CUT TO:

EXT. TRUCKING SCHOOL – YARD SCHOOL

Usually, I am the first guy to be at the battlefield.
If I go out to meet someone, I must be at the meeting place first. If I
go to a school, I must be there before everyone. I must conquer any
fear of the unknown. I'm there, I see the terrain, I start feeling
comfortable, there are no surprises after all. Then, whenever the
event begins, I will feel at home, ready for any kind of action.
This is some sort of pre-superhero condition.

So I'm waiting in the front yard of the CDL school, and Pavel
arrives ten minutes after me.
Pavel is a twenty-six-year-old Caucasian guy who is also attending
the CDL school.
I met him on the first day of school and he seemed nice enough,
even though he comes from Russia.

Ok, as long as he seems nice, I don't have any problem with where
he comes from. You know, once my capitalist mother said, "Just
because you came from your father's testicles, doesn't mean that
you are a dick. Just because you came from my vagina, doesn't
mean that you are a pussy. Just because you were born in the
hospital, doesn't mean that you are a doctor. Your chances to
become a nurse are higher, though. Just because you were born in a

place surrounded by ignorance, doesn't mean that you are ignorant. Just because you were born in an occupied place, doesn't mean that you are an American. You see, there is no reason to be proud of the place you come from, or to be a patriot, or racist, or religious, or ignorant. It all happened by chance, you have to illuminate."

When I asked her why she wouldn't divorce my communist father, since he has most of those flaws, she answered, "Because the illusion of love, has made more slaves than any king in history." And I think my mother loved Marilyn because she dared to divorce only after four years marriage.

Anyway, my mother was right, and Pavel really is a nice guy, even though he was born in Russia. He is also an American Citizen.

Pavel is walking toward me.

"Hey Pavel, Good morning."
"Good morning, Festim."
"How are you doing, man?"
"Good, good."
We shook hands, and he fished a pack of cigarettes out of his pocket and offered me one,
"You want a cigarette?"
"No, thanks, I don't smoke those."
He chuckled and said, "You don't smoke this?", and he put the cigarette between his lips and as he was lighting it up said, "What do you smoke?"
I smiled and I looked around and said, "You know what I smoke, good stuff."
"Good, good, here we go, welcome to Washington bro."
He gently punched my arm and continued, "So you have some?"
"No, I don't, I quit, in a way."
"What do you mean, you quit, in a way?"
"You know, the truck driving thing, we are not allowed."
"Fuck that shit, bro."
"No you don't fuck that shit, once they catch you, you're done. Bye, bye truck driving for the rest of your life."
"Take it easy bro, it's not like that."
"How is it, then?"

"Well there is something called *****, and any time after you smoke that good stuff, you can take it, or if a cop stops you, right then you'll have time to drink it, and your blood will be as pure as water from the rivers of heaven."

"You're not bullshitting me?"

"Google it, bro."

This guy is making me think things, and you know what? Sometimes you don't need to sacrifice anything in life, you just have to know the right way to do it. Thinking of a short cut, that's false, there are no short cuts. The way was there all the time, you just didn't see it, or you were afraid to follow it, or you were believing in something else.

"You got this *****?"

"Oh yes, bro."

"Where do you get it?"

"In the pharmacy, and the best part is that you don't need a prescription from a doctor."

Pavel inhaled smoke from his cigarette… into his lungs, affecting his blood and his brain, and he exhaled, but very little smoke came out of his mouth and nose. I thought to myself, how could I build some kind of machine that would suck carbon dioxide smoke in and filter it inside and let out very little of it.

Pavel is for sure the best guy I have met in the USA, so far.

No, I don't even think there is some conspiracy going on, why would he lie to me about something like this? Just because he was born in Russia? I don't think so. No, no, no. He is a nice guy, he is an artist, and there is no way he could be a Russian spy.

After all those thoughts in my head during a short pause between us, as I'm staring at the smoke coming out of his mouth I change the subject, and I ask Pavel, "Can you find me a car?"

"A car?"

"Yes, any kind of car, as long as it runs, I can give you a hundred dollars, for the whole month."

"Yeah? Let me think."

"I just need to be able to drive to school."

"Yeah, yeah, don't worry man, just let me think.", said Pavel.

He inhaled the carbon dioxide from his cigarette, feeding his lungs, blood and brain with that stuff, and said, smiling, "You know what, come with me today after we finish school, I have a friend who may be able to find you a car, and I have some good stuff, so we can have a good time."

Well, anything was better than going back to that shit-hole and listening to and smelling the farts of the old ladies. And I needed to have some fun. Still, something in my head was telling me to make sure that Pavel had the magic drink.

"Bro, I don't wanna be a pussy, or annoying, but I just wanna make sure."

"What, bro?"

"Does that magic drink really exist, and can I seriously buy it without a prescription from a doctor?"

"Yes bro, don't worry about that, why are you thinking so hard about this shit?"

"Because I had an experience, and I'm kind of confused."

"What experience?", asked Pavel as he exhaled very little smoke from his mouth.

Our story fades into the smoke.

FADING IN:

THIRD SEASON TWO 2

HELL SUMMER HELL

INT. SMOKE

Our screen is smoky, and our cameraman pulls back and as he is doing so, slowly we see that the smoke in our screen is smoke from a cigarette.

A nurse in front of the Pharmacy is smoking. A man walks inside the pharmacy.
This man is me. The camera closes in on my face, and my left eye is almost completely closed.
When I came to America a mosquito made in Pakistan laboratory bit me, and I almost lost my left eye. I thought people would judge me and think that I joined the Illuminati since moving to America, and I didn't like that prejudice so I went to the pharmacy.

I walked inside the pharmacy, and with a clear head, I stopped in front of the cash register.
I see the pharmacist doing nothing but looking inside her bar. She was playing a game on her phone and I'm thinking to myself, 'what would be the politest way to break the nurse's concentration'.

"Excuse me, miss." I said this phrase very gently, and she elevated her left eyebrow, stared at me, shook her head and rose up with a big smile on her face.

"Welcome, how may I help you?"

Wow, I was surprised at how well programed she was, you must have a lot of experience to change your mood like that. Her mood had gone from fuck off to welcome.

Anyway, "I need an antibiotic for my eye, may I purchase it please?"
"Do you have the prescription from the doctor?" she asked me
"No, do I need one? I mean, I know what I want."

"Yeah, but we are not allowed to sell you any kind of antibiotic without a doctor's prescription", another programed sentence came out of her mouth.

"So?"

"So, the doctor is right around the corner. You can go and visit her."

"All right, fair enough, see you shortly."

I walked to the other side of the store, and there on the door is written 'Doctor's Office', and in front of the door there is a touchscreen computer, where you have to check in and get a waiting number. The doctor will come out to see you shortly because you are not allowed to walk inside the doctor's office.

And I thought, another programmed patient doctor relationship, but I really didn't do any of the things I was supposed to do, so I poked my head inside the doctor's office and as soon as she saw that someone was sneaking inside her office without warning, I mean knocking on the door, she moved her laptop to another table, pretending that she was doing something, and again I broke her concentration on doing nothing.

"Excuse me, doctor", I rose my left hand to wave to her and I smiled.

And of course she elevated her left eyebrow and turned around with a big fake smile.

"Well, hello." She said.

I replied, "Hey", and she continued, "Did you sign in at the computer in front of the office?"

I looked back at the computer and then turned back to look at the doctor, and said "Oh, the computer? Yes, I saw it outside, but no, I didn't sign in, anyway I just have a small request."

She replied, "Well, okay, just wait for me outside, I'll be there shortly."

I said, "Okay, cool, thanks." And I moved outside in front of the touchscreen computer waiting for the doctor.

I guess shortly means about two minutes of waiting, because she came out after two minutes had gone by.

"Yes, how may I help you?"

"I just need a prescription for my eye."

"Well you have to sign in, and then I have to examine you."
"Sign in, then I have to pay right?" I replied and my smile faded away.
Her fake smile remained, "Do you have health insurance?"
I shook my head. "No."
"Then it's going to cost you one hundred dollars." She said, elevated her left eyebrow, and made her duck face lips to pretend she felt bad.
"I have to give you a hundred dollars, so I can get my medicine?" She was about to respond, but I continued with a louder tone, "What kind of thief are you?" she stepped back and I continued raising my tone.
"Who made this fucking rule? This means that I cannot heal myself because I can't pay you to prescribe my medicine."

The doctor was shaking, and I moved to the other side where I could get the medicine and I started yelling at the pharmacist who was behind the counter, "If I need a condom, does she need to measure the size of my dick so she can write a prescription for the condom?"

A complete silence came over the store, and for a second I wanted to believe in Jesus Christ and in his miracles, and out of nowhere a huge bright light came and shone on the store and Jesus appeared in front of me, and I went on my knees, and I started crying and Jesus gently laid his hand over my head, and for a quarter of the second that I was imagining Jesus, I thought of a blow job, and Jesus said to me, "I know what you're thinking son, don't worry, everything will be all right, now close your eyes", and I did, and Jesus continued "Oh dear father, help this…" and Jesus stopped his prayer and I opened my eyes and I looked at Jesus, and he looked at me suspiciously and asked me "Wait a minute, I didn't hear you earlier, do you have health insurance?"
"No, Jesus, no I don't." I answered crying and Jesus shook his head and said "Fuck", and he ran behind the counter where the pharmacists were and turned off the reflector that was shining on me, and screamed, "You fucking invader, you are wasting my time, get the fuck out of here, someone call the police please."

And I didn't know what the fuck was going on, but a knife that was on one of the shelves caught my eye, and I ran to it and grabbed it. I held the knife against my throat, took out my phone and was ready to live stream on Facebook. I said to them "How about now, bitches? I'll stream my suicide live on Facebook what will your future look like? Fuck that Hippocratic oath, and obey the hypocrite oath."

Then Jesus, the pharmacists and the doctor saw that I was serious about committing suicide, and Jesus screamed, "Hey you fucking invader, here is what you want. Come get it."
And I walked slowly with the knife held to my throat, took the medicine, and I asked how much and Jesus said the price plus the tax.

And that is how I got my medicine. Did I ever tell you that I finished four years of medical high school, and finished three years of medical college back in my country and here, suddenly, nothing is the same? Just like how the formula for water is H2O everywhere else but here it's HBO.

After I took the medicine I walked outside and the guy was still smoking outside in front of the store and above his head was a 'No Smoking' sign. Dogs, guns, and knives are allowed inside." I thought about smoking the dogs and guns, but I couldn't see how you could smoke a knife.

The guy in front of the store puffed out some smoke and our screen fades into…

INT. PAVEL'S SMOKING ROOM – NIGHT

I mean this is what you call a smoking room. You could blind one of your friends with your finger if he could see your finger from the smoke that was made inside this room.
It's very difficult to see us laying on the ground and smoking.
It's I, Festim. Pavel and his friend are having a good time on the ground in the middle of the room, and are higher than the seven heavens together.

"You gave me an idea man!" said Pavel

"What's that?" I asked

"…for example, designers, people who make clothes, they make some deal with the government like the same way that doctors have deals with governments and insurance companies, and just like you said, in here you cannot cure yourself, but designers, you cannot wear yourself. You need a personal designer in order to look good and be beautiful, and this would be for the greater good of the city. All of the city would look beautiful. Think about that! It's a win-win, one of you opens a good looking insurance company, and the artist, in this case me, is the guy in charge of making the clothes. I'd dress this city in purple grey charcolate with small pink bubbles and tine yellow stripes with shape of feather."

We were still forming his master plan when Pavel's friend started laughing loudly, and we joined in his laughter and the three of us were all laughing out loud (LOL). And then we stopped, and Pavel's friend said "Now I see how high they were when they made those rules about health insurance", and we started laughing again. After that laugh there was a long silence, and then I fished my phone out of my pocket and I looked at the time, and the time was gone, I couldn't find it, so I brought my phone closer to my eyes and now I could see it.

10:00 P.M.

I got up, took the keys for my new car, and I thanked the guys for the car and for the good time and they said Spasciba, too.

As I opened the door, Pavel told me to be careful on the road and to buckle up, "because you don't have insurance and it will cost a lot if something happens… and even if you have insurance, you better put your fucking seat belt on, because the police will write you a ticket. It's not about that bullshit safety thing, no, no, no, they don't care about that, it's because if you get hurt it'll cost the insurance companies money."

I thought that it was never about us, and Pavel said it's all about their profit.

Pavel is a true, nice guy.

Word of the day:

1. Legal
2. Good
3. Illegal
4. Bad
5. Mediocre

Sentence of the day:
Good marijuana should be legal, but bad marijuana should be illegal, and this is a mediocre thought.

CUT TO:

CUT TO:

INT. LEVIN'S HOUSE – MORNING

White subtitles in the middle of a black screen.

Seven days at Levin's house.

While we are still in a black screen we hear the shower begin to run
and slowly our screen shows an image of Festim taking a shower.

> FESTIM (V.O)
> Everything is fine now, I'm going to
> school to learn how to truck-drive,
> and here in the house I found a
> solution. I salute the old ladies, but I
> don't do anything more than that, I
> only salute AZOBO as well.
> I guess with retired people all you
> have to do is let them go, and, no need
> to worry, they will not hurt anyone.
> Precisely. In my system they do no
> harm. They are like water that goes
> down the drain, nothing stops it, or
> hurts it.

FESTIM turns off the water, takes his towel, dries
himself off and puts on clothes. He goes upstairs to
get his bag and car keys, comes downstairs and goes
to the dining table to salute the ladies.

> FESTIM
> Good morning.

> VERA
> You should eat with us, sometimes.

FESTIM walks backward two steps, stops, and says,

FESTIM
Yeah you're right, I promise tonight I
will join you for dinner.

He walks outside, thinking.

Fade out:

Fade in:

EXT: STARBUCKS – SAME DAY – AFTERNOON

FESTIM is walking into Starbucks.

INT: STARBUCK

FEESTIM has a medium cup of coffee in his hand
and is looking for a place to sit.

On his cup of coffee the name "JOHN" is written.

FESTIM sees the pictures on the walls, and the sweet
slaves working in the fields are happy and are
smiling for all of us, we who buy their coffee and
never think about how much they get paid per day,
something like 1$.
Well I really think about how artistic pictures the
photographer sized.

Thoughts like that don't come about very often.

Festim sees a beautiful woman sitting alone holding
an open book with an iPhone in the middle of the
book. The cup of coffee on her table reads, 'ANNA'.

FESTIM walks toward her and takes a seat at her
table.

She stares at him, wondering what he's doing.

FESTIM puts his coffee on the table and says,

> FESTIM
> I apologize; I didn't ask you if this seat
> is free, or if I could sit here.
> But I'm wondering if you have ever
> bought a drink and found a beautiful
> view and wanted to sit in front of the
> beautiful view to enjoy your drink
> while you admire it?

The woman puts the book on the table, smiles, and
speaks softly with an Eastern European accent,

> THE WOMAN
> It would be funny if the view would
> ask you, 'Why are you staring at me?'
>
> You can sit… and thank you for the
> compliment.

> FESTIM
> You are very welcome.
> Where are you from? I hear your
> accent.

> THE WOMAN
> Serbia. You?

> FESTIM
> And what's your name?

> THE WOMAN
> JELENA

> FESTIM
> FESTIM

FESTIM stretches his hand to shake hands with
JELENA.

JELENA slowly gives her hand.

FESTIM holding her hand says.

                    FESTIM
          Nice to meet you, I am your enemy,
          JELENA, I come from Albania, from
          Kosovo.

                    JELENA
          Ahhh, nice.

                                        CUT TO:

INT: LEVIN'S HOUSE – SAME DAY - NIGHT

On the right side of our screen, we see FESTIM in the
hallway on his bed, banging JELENA, and on the left
side we can see the stairs and a little bit of the
hallway.

After twenty seconds, we hear ROSA.

                    ROSA (O.S)
                    (Very laud)
          JESUS, Jesus, Jesus Christ, Hallelujah,
          Hallelujah, Hallelujah!

ROSA is on the screen, shown at the bottom of the
stairs. She has both hands raised high and continues
singing.

                    ROSA
          Hallelujah, Hallelujah…

FESTIM continues banging JELENA.

> **JELENA**
> Oh yeah, ohhhh, fuck… ohh bozhe
> yeahhh…

> **FESTIM**
> Ohhh, yeahh, ohhh,,,,,,

> **ROSA**
> Hallelujah, …

> **JELENA**
> Ouuuu, fuuuuck, yeahhh…

                              DISOLVE TO:

INT: LEVIN'S HOUSE – SAME NIGHT

Subtitles on the screen read:

"15 minutes later."

Now we see only FESTIM and JELENA.

They are on the bed, staring at each other.

JELENA gets up and puts on her clothes…

> **JELENA**
> I have to go now. I'm glad that I met a
> nice Albanian.

> **FESTIM**
> My pleasure.

They both walk slowly down the stairs in silence, looking around and making sure that none of the old ladies would scare them.

EXT: STREET – SAME NIGHT

FESTIM and JELENA are kissing on the street.

They stop, and JELENA smiles and walks to the other side of the street without saying a word as FESTIM watches her, and we have a C.U. of FESTIM's eyes widened open.

FESTIM (V.O)

Good morning.
Last night Jelena and I had sex.
Where we come from we are sworn enemies. Funny huh?
No matter where enemies meet, they'll always try to fuck each other, one way or another. Even in America.
Or maybe, America is the place where enemies make love?! And this fucking thing… we're all taking it the wrong way....

CUT TO:

INT: LEVIN'S HOUSE – SAME NIGHT

FESTIM opens the front door, walks slowly inside, and closes the door.

When he turns around, MONA is behind him standing like a statue.

FESTIM becomes scared and starts to breathe heavily.

MONA
You missed your dinner tonight.

Word of the day:

1. Jelena
2. Sex
3. Kiss
4. Jelena
5. Again

Sentence of the day:

Let's make love.

CUT TO:

INT: LEVIN'S HOUSE – DINING ROOM – MORNING

7 in the morning, and Azobo was following his routine with the trays, and preparing food for the ladies.
That morning, I was sitting with the old ladies at the dining room table, and it was so boring.
Fast-forward, and thirty minutes later Azobo brings all the trays to the table, and as usual the ladies don't eat or take their pills.
Azobo takes a seat and starts eating. I've almost finished my food.

Azobo looks at Mona and tells her, "Mona eat, your friend is here, don't leave him alone."
He means me… I'm Mona's friend. I look at him and continue eating my food.

It didn't take too long for Azobo to finish his food. Afterward he took his tray and went back to the kitchen, and then came back and began his routine of getting the old ladies to eat and take their pills. The first lady he picked this time was Shellie. Azobo went to her chair and took the spoon and tried to feed her "Miss Shellie, come on, one sip, one sip, three sip, let's finish your soup" said Azobo as he tried to feed Shellie.

I looked at him and the rhythm at which I'd been eating began to slow down, and my nerves were getting fucked little by little.

Azobo opened the Shellie's mouth, shoveled her pills in, and gave her the glass of water, all the while telling her, "Now take the pills, they keep you alive. Good, water, water, water… nice…" and I couldn't take my eyes off of Shellie. She was staring at me, begging for help.

Azobo finished with Shellie and moved on to Veronica. He started doing the same thing, telling her, "Veronica my dear, you been good today, you finished your food, just the pills now. Opa, opa, open your mouth." And he took the pills, put them in her mouth and, with force, gave her the water. In that moment I interrupted, "Hey man, take it easy with ladies, don't force them." Azobo gave me a look that said, 'What the fuck?" and continued his routine.

He took the Shellie and Veronica's trays and brought them back to the kitchen and came back to continue his routine with Mona. He took the pills and said, "Mona, come on, opa, finish your pills." and he opened Mona's mouth, but Mona moved her head to the side and closed her mouth. Azobo grabbed Mona by her chin, brought her head towards his face and tried to open her mouth with force, and I woke up and pushed Azobo and told him not to touch the ladies anymore, they don't want the pills.

He replied, "First, you don't touch me, and second, she is going to die if she don't take the pills. This is my job, to keep her alive." He opened Mona's mouth and shoveled the pills in, and I pushed him and screamed at him "You motherfucker don't touch her, she doesn't want the fucking pills."
He stood up and said to me, pointing his long index finger, "Listen to me well, I'm taking care for the ladies, if they don't take the medicine they will die."
"So why do you care if they die or not?
"This is my job, and you don't put your nose in my job, I will talk to Levin today."

Mona spit out the pill on the table, and Azobo walked upstairs to the second floor.

It was the time for me to leave and go to school, so I took my bag and I dove deep into thought as I left the house, and this chapter of my life I called Chapter 84: Boring time with old people.
Yeah you can skip this chapter, because it's the boring chapter, and very soon this is going to be your life. I'm positive about your negative future, because you're wasting too much time on entertainment and self-soothing, or maybe your life is already boring.
Can you google it?
I have good news, dude. Don't worry, because Azobo is there to keep you alive, even if you'd give your most precious possessions to die when your life gets boring.
Your life.
I give you my life to kill me.
Yeah, I know that, but Azobo can't make a living with your dead life, he needs your life to be alive. That's the only way he can get paid.
And then I see all this scene as a movie scene and…

He is thinking.

> FESTIM (V.O)
> I'm very sorry for the old ladies, but I cannot do anything to help them. If I call the cops and tell them what's going on, then fuck my CDL. LEVIN will say that I stole his address and that I don't even live there, and I'll have to go back to one of the shitty jobs that I hated. This means taking a detour and rerouting my destiny. I wish I could find another short-cut to reach my dream.

FESTIM takes his bag, walks downstairs, opens the front door and walks outside.

Camera keeps following FESTIM for ten more feet, then the camera stops and takes a 180 degree turn. We see AZOBO close the door, and we can hear from inside:

                    VERONICA (S.O)
                      (Screaming)
          Help me, help me…

Camera moves fast towards the door, but the door is locked, so the camera moves to the right side to the window.

Suddenly, VERONICA hits the window with her palm and screams.

                    VERONICA
          Help me, help me.

VERONICA starts crying and shrieking.

VERONICA slowly starts to calm down and think.

                                    FADE OUT:

FADE IN:

EXT.STREET - DAY

FESTIM goes to school.

We see FESTIM on CU walking outside, and we understand that he's thinking about the ladies and that house.

On our screen comes short scenes, snapshots of moments in the house.

AZOBO opening MONA's mouth.

ROSA singing Hallelujah.

We see FESTIM thinking.

                                        Cut TO:

INT: TRUCK SCHOOL – CLASS ROOM

FESTIM is thinking.

                    INSTRUCTOR (S.O)
            FESTIM, are you listening?

FESTIM turns back to reality.

                        FESTIM
            Oh yeah, yeah…

INSTRUCTOR chuckles as he shows
how to work with a piece of
machinery in the truck.

                    INSTRUCTOR
            I was saying that you have to force it
            to open…

                                        CUT TO:

Memory when AZOBO tells MONA to open her
mouth..

                        AZOBO
            …open your mouth MONA.

                                        CUT TO:

EXT: STREET – AFTERNOON – SUNSET

FESTIM walking on the street towards LEVIN's house.

FESTIM (V.O)
All day, I thought about the ladies. I didn't feel good all day.

CUT TO:

Black screen white letters in the middle of the screen:

FOURTH SEASON FOUR 4

NORMALLY WINTER IS COLD
THE COLD IS NOT NORMAL IF IT FREEZES YOUR HEART

That night, once I was home from school, I saw a beautiful girl sitting with Mona at the dining room table. I guess she didn't see me, so I went into the kitchen and pretended I was doing something, while I tried to figure out who this beautiful woman that was spending time with Mona was.

It didn't take too long. Mona soon asked her, "How are the dogs, my dear?"
I began to listen intently, and the woman answered, "Oh they are good, the new one is so spoiled… I've been showing him so much love that Jane is starting to get very jealous…" and then I hear the sound of a ringtone coming from the dining room.
"Oh I got a text from Jennifer… my puppy is not feeling good. I have to go mom. Goodbye, I love you." She said, and she ran out of the house.

What the fuck? What the fuck was that puppy thing? And who was she? Did she just say, bye mom? I slowly walked out of the kitchen and went to the dining room table, and there I saw Mona sitting alone in her chair. I took another chair and sat and looked at Mona, wondering, and finally I spoke, "Who was she? Your daughter?"

She nodded, and I continued with my speech, "Mona after what happened earlier, I was feeling very sad all day thinking about you, about how this asshole is treating you, and, I hate to say it Mona, but, after everything that happens in this shitty house, you can still think about your daughter's dogs? I mean, what the fuck Mona? Please don't tell me that Jennifer is her dog-sitter. This is insane that she has time for her dogs and that she had money to pay someone to watch her dogs, but she sent you here and barely visits you. This is fucked up... or maybe it's just what American families do. Did you do the same thing to your parents? Did you treat them like shit for some filthy animals Mona? Tell me? The apple doesn't fall far from the tree. You know what? I'm starting to feel sorry for the Nigerian man that is taking care of you. I bet he left his family to come here and work, just to send some food back to his home. But you, right here in this moment, you are fucked. You deserve to live like this."

And we just lost our minds.
Within me, everything is cracking and breaking apart.
Nothing makes sense.

We fade to black.

Everything is blurry, smoky, dark, silent, far, mixed, confused, and lost.

I was just a child when my father tried to plant his ideas into my head. He wanted to make me believe that nationalism should dwell in my heart and mind, and that we all have to give our lives when it comes to our country and to god. Every day, he would surround me with figures and colors that represented his ideologies. I always tried to close my eyes and my ears, my receptor senses, in order to block all of this out.
You know, brainwashing has nothing to do with removing your memory and installing a completely different software. Typically, brainwashing has to do with controlling the bridges that connect the outside world to our receptors and our inside world.

Building intelligent army punkts on those bridges, and controlling what kind of information can go through and what not.

Is that Kim's ass? Oh, I know those boobs! And *those* tits. I came a few times thinking of those sweaty boobs. Crazy me, right? People loved Marilyn, because porn wasn't popular back in time.

Fuck. Hell, I don't get it, what is the media trying to implant into my mind with all those asses and tits, abs and dicks?!
Can somebody help me?
Or maybe it's just trying to keep me busy as it plots against me.
Why me? Did I do something? I didn't do anything wrong. I just wanted to come to America.
I even killed my communist father for you… for democracy.
How?
Before I left my home, I strapped him in his chair in his room, I installed five large speakers inside the room, and I played Frank Sinatra's 'New York, New York'. That song would play over, and over, and over again, for the rest of his life, and he would die of starvation and dehydration, listening to the music he hated most.
Franz Kafka is lobbying in the corridors of the heavenly clouds with angels to save a nice lazy sofa for me when I transcendent there.
Am I dreaming? Or am I feeling sick in pain? Or am I just completely lost?
I'm feeling sick in pain and lost in the American Dream.
For a starter my doctor gave me few pain killers. Bad news, pain killers destroy those bridges that connect the disease with the cure. Worse news, we didn't locate the problem yet. Witch Hunter. Brainwashing. Then my doctor prescribed me so called Exchange Lifestyle. I guess he was meaning to take the life of someone else, because my life was already ruined. So I started killing people trying to take their life, but hell, once I shoot them, their life is gone. And again I'm a looser, lost in the American Dream.
When you are lost and there is nothing left to say, what do you say? Disarmed and lost in this game, unwillingly, out of my mouth came the word, "Nothing".
"Correct answer, and we have a winner!" exclaimed the jury, and the dancers began dancing and flashing their boobs at me, ready to give me a lap dance. The crowd went crazy, screaming and

shouting my name, and I was feeling good, heavenly, even. Lighter than the sun and the feather.

And I read in the sky, "A capitalist and a dictator are the same. They'll both kill you on behalf of the people. And dear God, above in the sky, is watching and wondering why the fuck he can't be a part of this game. He is completely powerless and submerged in thought, with his arms crossed he is shaking his enormous head." My father finished his sentence, and I asked him if I really look like I care about his theories.

I just wanted to come to America.

And I woke up roaring like a lion, or screaming like a scared man, holding my head, in pain and frustrated from the dream, or the nightmare, that I just saw.

I stand up, not sure if I'm sleep walking or really awake.

I walk downstairs and enter the kitchen. On the wall is a list of the names and the information of the ladies in this house. As I look at their names and their information, like addresses, and their sickness and inabilities, I saw a name of someone that I had not heard of.

DEA ISDESH

What kind of a name is that? I wanted to take a picture of this list, but I didn't have my phone with me, and I thought to myself that I must be sleep walking, otherwise I would have had my phone on me; I don't go to take a piss without my phone, you know, that's the only friend I've got. So what am I doing in front of this list? Oh... I remove the list from the wall, fold it up, and shove it in my pocket.

I hear voices to my left, and I see that it's the TV. Kill Bill is playing, and Budd is telling Bill, "Those ladies deserve their revenge and their kids deserve to die."

I shook my head in disbelief, and in my left ear I heard, "Peace is boring, but war is one hell of an entertainment" and I look him in the blind eyes and give him an evil smile and he asks me, "So what is it going to be Vanilla boy?"

We're going to have a lot of fun.

Now that's my superhero name ---------------------------------------
>>>>>>>>   Vanilla boy

I open my eyes.

This time I was awake for real and I know this because my phone is beside my head. When I see my phone next to me, it's small blue light blinking, telling me that I have notifications, I grab it. Of course, the first thing I do in the morning is check my notifications, and as soon as I click the home button to see everything, a picture of a list pops up on my screen. It's the same list I saw last night, with the same name written in capital letters:

DEA ISDESH

                                                            CUT TO:

REPENTANCE and VENGEANCE at their finest

This is my index finger, and that is a door bell. I will push it now…
ding-dong, ding-dong… a short pause, and again, ding-dong, ding-
dong.
Through the door's eye I look different now, and not just because of
the convexity of the door's eye, but because I've changed my look
entirely.
I'm no more Norma Jean Baker.
I'm Vanilla boy
The door opens to reveal Mona's daughter who smiles and says,
"Hi."
I've cleaned myself up to look like a doctor, clean shaven, hair
slicked back with gel. I look like I just came out of the shower.
"Good afternoon, I'm Doctor Frederic Bah, and I'm here regarding
your mother's condition."
Mona's daughter's eyes widen.
"What happened to my mother? Is she all right?"
Just as she was about to ask another question, she was interrupted
by two small yappy dogs that had ran to her side.
I thought about my father's dog for less than a second and then
came back to reality. She asked me to enter, and that's all I had
wanted.
We sat at her dining room table, and the puppies began to run all
over the house.
My nerves began their protest.
"So doctor what happened to my mother?" asked this beautiful
lady.
I fished out from my back a smooth, shiny Glock and pointed it at
her. Her dogs jumped up onto her lap knowing that something was
about to happen, and I see myself in her eyes. In this moment, she's
facing her archangel.
"Listen bitch, I heard you want to be some kind of movie star.
Maybe you will be one day, but don't be like one of those stupid
women in movies…" and she interrupted me with what sounded
like half of a voice, "I didn't do anything…"
"Listen you stupid bitch, I'm telling you not to become one of those
stupid women from the movies that doesn't listen when the smart

man, in our scene, me, tells you to do something, because that's when bad things happen because of poor decisions."

Again, she opened her mouth to say something, and this is the first time in her life that her mouth was open and yet, at the same time, it's zipped. There is silence; no words make their way out because I've shoved my gun in her mouth and her subconscious is telling her to keep her cool.

"The person who sent me to kill you is a very generous person, you would never believe who this person is, and because she is a great mother, I should do something better than murder her stupid, little daughter." I'm giving my murder speech to Mona's daughter and she starts crying. The tears from her eyes wash the outside of the barrel of my gun and I wonder what kind of a reaction could happen when her tears meet the iron.

I continue with my speech after what was a short pause for me, but felt like an eternity for her, "When your mother hears that I killed your stupid dogs in front of you, and that I cooked them and ate them, she'll be more than…" I stopped and I thought that I should come up with a better speech, then I continued, "Your mother loves you very much, and she dares to bomb the entire world just to live in her home, in this house with her daughter, but her daughter is such a disappointment. She thinks she can justify her actions with the thought that she can't afford to, but bitch, I know you have the ability to take care of your mother. I know that you have enough money to pay for someone to take care of her when you're not around, but you are just a disgusting, miserable, filthy, selfish, child of the world and…" I pulled the trigger, unwillingly, and blew off her head, the blood spreading all around, and I shot the first puppy and then the second, while they were still in shock over the scene they just witnessed, not leaving them the chance to bark for help.

I wished that I could wake up, but I was already awake.

True sanity within insanity, dwells only in people with great dreams.

And CUT TO:

INT: LEVIN'S HOUSE – AFTERNOON

Inside the dark room, a room that I have never been in inside Levin's house, there lives a secret. I decided to call the room, The Secret Room of DEA ISDESH.
Our cameraman is shooting two black oily hands. It's dark, and those hands are running over a body that remains unknown.
The black hands grab a bottle of oil and pour the oil over that body gently, spreading the oil over this naked body and we cannot see the body's color, because it's dark and hazy.

Our screen dissolves again, and we are inside of Levin's house in the living room.
We can see Levin and Azobo talking to each other. Levin is the first to start the conversation, "Did you finish with her?"
"Yes, everything is good, just like you told me." replied Azobo, and Levin continued with his questions.
"So you fed the ladies and you cleaned them?"
"Actually the new guy caused a problem today. He wouldn't let me feed Mona and he blocked me from giving her the pills." said Azobo and Levin screamed at him, "What? Are you stupid? You must give them their pills, if they miss a meal every now and then, it's fine, but the pills, they keep them alive."
"Yeah, I know."
"Yeah, you don't know. If you knew, you would do as I say. You know that if one of them dies I'll cut off the payment? Only if they are alive you get the money."
"Okay, but you better talk to the boy."
"He needs my address, and he needs to stay somewhere. I'll talk to him, he will keep his mouth shut and his eyes closed, don't worry. I'm going to church now, with my family. See you later."

Good, good, good, and cut:

FIFTH SEASON FIVE 5

Chaos. The word is typical, but, as a fact is a lack of control, or, you had more than two beers.

FADE IN:

INT: LEVIN'S HOUSE

The house looks pretty calm for the moment.

FESTIM is in the kitchen pouring milk into a glass.

AZOBO takes a small cup with three pills inside, walks out to the kitchen, and serves the cup of pills to SHELLY.

AZOBO says nothing to SHELLY, he just leaves the cup in front of her and goes upstairs.

All of the ladies are sitting in their chairs.

ROSA wakes up and starts doing her laps from the mirror to the dining room table.

SHELLY takes the cup and examines it.

                    SHELLY (V.O)
          Everything in this house is so shallow,
          just like this cup with these three
          frozen pills. I named them, pain,
          loneliness and uncaring, and they
          stand together hand by hand in this
          shallow cup. I'll take the three of
          them, every day and they give me
          another day, another day, another
          day.
          They were meant to cure people by
          the way.
          But another day for me means three
          more things that I don't want to have.

Most of the time I don't want another
day, but they are meant to cure people
by the way.

SHELLY (con't)
I don't want another day, but they are
meant to cure people by the way. I
don't want another day, but they are
meant to cure people by the way. I
don't want another day, but they are
meant to cure people by the way...

As ROSA is doing her laps, suddenly, like her soul
escaped from her body, she loses control and falls to
the ground.

FESTIM was drinking his milk and thinking. He
looks up to see what happened and sees ROSA on
the ground.

VERA
Nothing is going the way I want this
year...

SHELLY doesn't stop repeating herself,

SHELLY
I don't want another day.............

Camera freezes the scene and we hear
FESTIM

FESTIM (V.O)
Fuck. Do I help her, or not? Or do I
call an ambulance.
If I help she might try to claim that I
dislocated her neck or arm or
whatever and sue me...

FESTIM takes a step back and stops…

> FESTIM (V.O)
> …if I don't help, this ain't human at
> all. Fuck. I'll call the ambulance.

FESTIM, on the same foot that he took a step back with,
takes a step forward and stops..

> FESTIM
> Wait… I didn't sign up for this shit.
> It's not my Job.

Rosa's body starts shaking like she's being possessed
and…

> FESTIM
> Fuck this shit.

FESTIM screams and runs towards
ROSA

> FESTIM
> AZOBO, help me, ROSA is on the
> ground, ROSA is on the ground! Call
> the ambulance!!

FESTIM opens ROSA's mouth and pulls her tongue
out so she won't swallow it.

SHELLY continues with her repetition…

The other ladies gather around ROSA, just staring at
her, doing nothing.

VERA gives her opinion.

> VERA
> We should take the bus.

VERA looks at the ladies, bows her head and says,

                    VERA
          I'm sorry, I forgot. The bus doesn't
          run on Saturday.

                    MONA
          Why? Are they Jewish?

                    VERA
          I don't know.

When FESTIM called to AZOBO to call an
ambulance, we hear AZOBO running and the camera
is in position to see the kitchen, the dining room table
and the stairs.

                    AZOBO
                  (screaming)
          Don't call the ambulance, don't call
          the ambula-…

AZOBO slips and slides down the
stairs on his ass.

AZOBO, at the end of the stairs, is holding his back
and groaning.

                    FESTIM
          Oh shit, I'm calling an ambulance.
                  (to the old ladies)
          One of you bring me a phone.

VERA takes the remote control and stretches her
hand to give it to FESTIM.

FESTIM chuckles, takes the remote control with one
hand, and with the other holds ROSA's tongue.

                    FESTIM
Thank you VERA, but there's no
service on this one.

FESTIM sees the phone in the kitchen.

AZOBO is still groaning and can't
move.

FESTIM quickly stands up and runs to the kitchen.
He grabs the phone, runs back, and opens ROSA's
mouth to pull out her tongue again.

FESTIM presses the buttons for 911, and calls them.

                    AZOBO
              (Barely speaks)
Don't call an ambulance, it will cost
three thousand dollars, no one will
pay for her and LEVIN will kill both
of us.

                  911 (S.O)
911, where is your emergency?

                    FESTIM
What?

                    AZOBO
Hang up, hang up. I can help her.

FESTIM hangs up.

                    FESTIM
What? Did you say three thousand
dollars for an ambulance?

                    AZOBO
Yes, with all expenses for her.

                    FESTIM
Why? What does she need?

                    AZOBO
An I.V.

                    FESTIM
An I.V?

                    AZOBO
Yes.

                    FESTIM
Three thousand dollars for an I.V?

                    AZOBO
A thousand dollars for the ambulance,
100 to 150 for an I.V, plus the time of
the Doctor and Nurse.

                    FESTIM
Fucking stop here.

In our show, everyone freezes except
FESTIM.

FESTIM stands up, talking. He walks to the kitchen,
takes a bottle of water and NACL, puts some salt in
the water, and mixes it.

                    FESTIM
Real chaos is when Prada, Gucci, and
Louie Vuitton sell their products
cheaper than the doctor sells you an
I.V.
An I.V cost **1$ + tax = 1.15$.**

Now an I.V contains nothing more or
less than water and NACL or house
salt plus… wait, who gives a fuck
what it contains, we all have THE
GOOD LOOKING INSURANCE. But
seriously just think about this, a nurse,
plus an I.V, plus five minutes for her
to come, plus five more minutes for
her to finish her job equals a thousand
dollar. This is the most expensive
escort company I have ever heard of.

This is out of the Script-Dream-Nightmare.
Hell, I'm not even exercising and I'm thinking about what my
Democratic-Capitalist mother once told me. She said that I must
become a doctor, and I know she was a wonderful mother, she
wouldn't ever tell me to do something stupid or evil. I knew that
when she told me to become a doctor, she meant that she wanted
me to help people, not to kill them or to give them pain killers that
will never truly cure them so they'll forever remain my clients. I
knew her, she was open minded. Her idol was Marilyn Monroe, not
Stalin.
Or, or, or… wait, I have a bad idea right now about my mother.
I don't know if I should share this with you, but maybe, perhaps,
because she was open-minded, she wanted me to become one of
those thieves who claim to be doctors. Perhaps, she knew
capitalism's whole plan, and she knew that we wouldn't have a
chance to escape from it, so she wanted me to be a successful part of
it. Maybe she never told me this because she knew that Capitalism
is shit for society, and she wanted to transfer the burden of guilt
over my shoulders.
She told me to become a doctor so I could not blame her later when
I dissolve into a predator, a capitalistic blood sucker, sucking
money out of sick people.
She always knew that it was all about money, that it had nothing to
do with being altruistic.
My fucking mother, that slut, whore, bitch.
I dared to justify not helping Rosa because of her… because I didn't
sign up for that, because it wasn't my job.

Exactly, this is not a job or a contract to sign in, this is a human life.
This is a real problem that I must fix it.
Stupid, fuck me. Idiot.
How badly in my brain did my mother and father imbed those
fucked up, shitty ideas. They were the only ones fucking in our
family. Fucking parents.

FESTIM walks back to the position he was in before,
where he was holding ROSA's tongue.

AZOBO is still groaning.

VERA goes into the kitchen, opens one of the shelves,
fishes out an I.V. and the injections, and shows it to
FESTIM.

> VERA
> Are you looking for this, son?

FESTIM nods his head and replies to VERA.

> FESTIM
> Oh yes, please bring it here.

> VERA
> Is this what you need? Poor ROSA,
> this was here for so many days. She is
> dead now.

VERA turns toward the shelves and slowly tries to
put the I.V. and the injections back on the shelf.

FESTIM shakes his head.

> FESTIM
> No, no, she is not dead, Vera. Please
> bring that here.

> VERA
> She is not dead?

                        FESTIM
              No, she's not. Come here.

VERA leaves the I.V. and the injection on the shelf.

She closes the shelf, turns towards FESTIM with a
smile on her face, and starts walking toward him.

                        FESTIM
              Bring that I.V. here VERA.

                        VERA
              Was that an order?

FESTIM bows his head and shakes it, and then asks
MONA to help him.

                        FESTIM
              MONA, MONA, would you please
              hold ROSA's tongue for me?

                        MONA
              Absolutely, yes.

MONA bows and grabs the tongue of ROSA.

FESTIM holds ROSA in his arms.

MONA is still holding her tongue while FESTIM
puts ROSA on the bed.

FESTIM goes in the kitchen and takes the I.V. and the
injection off the shelf.

VERA stares at FESTIM.

FESTIM walks toward ROSA, and VERA moves to block his way. When FESTIM tries to pass by VERA, she grabs his shoulder…

                    VERA
          Why didn't you ask me to bring you
          the I.V.? Do you think that I'm useless
          and inhuman, and cannot help those
          in need?

                    FESTIM
          Okay VERA, then help me to help her,
          and please go and bring me that
          hanger pool.

FESTIM pointed at the "hanger pool" behind the door.

FESTIM walked toward ROSA and began to prepare the I.V.

VERA grabs the hanger, walks toward FESTIM, and leaves the hanger pool next to ROSA's head.

FESTIM is preparing the I.V. and giving it to ROSA.

                    VERA
          I knew it from the beginning that
          you're a doctor.
          (short pause)

People like you have discovered the
new sickness, they called it
Doctorizing, and the patients who are
infected with this disease are called
Predators, because those Predators
call their prey PATIENT. The way of
killing the prey depends on the
strength, weakness, and mental
condition of the prey.

VERA then stops speaking and vanishes, and, at that
same moment, FESTIM finishes with the I.V.

He gives a sigh of relief, bows his head and begins
talking to himself.

                    FESTIM (V.O.)
          Hooo… I did it.

FESTIM raises his head and, while looking at the
stairs, his face contorts in suspicion.

Camera shoots AZOBO laying at the bottom of the
stairs, passed out.

We hear FESTIM.

                    FESTIM (O.S.)
          VERA, do you have another I.V.
          somewhere around here?
                                        CUT TO:

SIXTH SEASON

TRUE INSPIRATION COMES THROUGH TRUE EVENTS, wait…
Does this mean that FAKE events like barbeques and parties with
friends of friends, nightclubs, one night stands … bring
FAKEYTALES?

After school, Pavel and I would usually go eat Thai food.
I loved Chicken Teriyaki, and Pavel would eat something different.
The funny thing about that place was the picture of Jesus on the
wall behind the register. For almost two weeks, I went to that same
place and never noticed the picture on the wall, located between the
menu. I guess I was hungry. I thought that if Jesus represents 'Love'
and that the menu on the wall represented 'Hunger', might this
mean that the need to satisfy Hunger is greater than the need for
Love? It was just my thought, but, if you read the works of Sigmund
Freud, he says that Hunger represents the preservation of an
individual, and Love represents the preservation of an entire
species. Again, I think about whether this is why people decide to
self-sooth, subconsciously thinking that this is the way to preserve
their 'I self'.
For example, some Americans have evolved in a way that they
would rather feed a Chihuahua, a dog, than a Mexican, a human.
And this has nothing to do with racism, it has a self-soothing
purpose; do you remember my father and his puppy? Exactly.

Anyway, Pavel and I are having lunch, and Pavel is sort of a writer,
and he told me that he was writing something about illegal
immigration. I asked him to tell me some jokes, and he said,
"Okay, Arnold Schwarzenegger is on trial to either get a green card
or be deported back to Austria, and the judge decides to have him
deported. He tells him, "You have to go back in time, to Austria"
and Arnold says, "I'll be back."
I laughed because it was an okay joke, and I wanted to encourage
him so I told him it was very funny, but I didn't understand why he
was into writing jokes and stories about immigration. He told me
that he was not only writing for immigrants, but also for all of
humanity. With immigrants, however, he was trying to show that it
doesn't matter where we were born, we can't divide ourselves and

label ourselves as nationalists, religious, whatever, the only thing that should identify us is what we do in this life. Are we really helping one another? Or are we trying to feed into our own selfishness and jerk off every day when we feel low, instead of spending that jerking energy on something valuable… and just like Pavel, my mother would think the same.

But really, his jokes were mediocre and I thought I could help him with some inspiration. So I asked him if he wanted to come with me to a place that would help inspire him. I told him it would open gates in his head that he never thought he'd be able to pass through. He was positive, and said yes. I thought about how an illegal invader is a prisoner of his or her dream.

No matter how much everything can be twisted and become a nightmare, I can't escape from it, because it's the only hope I have in my life. I think about a suicide bomber. I think about how crazy sick he is when he comes to America with plans to destroy his dream. Fucking stupid. This is the only place you can be anything that you'd ever wanted to be.
Yeah, even a murderer. A suicide bomber.
'Anything' means murderer too, but that's just not right, and we all know it, right? But… to become a murderer you don't need to leave the place you were born, you can start with your family, your friends, neighbors and so on. So basically, what this tells me is that, if you travel to another place to kill people, you have no respect for yourself and you are a big piece of shit; a waste, garbage of the earth.

"Did you know that the word LIFE read backwards is SHIT?" I asked Pavel, and he raised his eyebrows and looked at the ceiling, thinking and reading backwards.

"Yes, actually, it is SHIT. Fuck, man. I never thought about that".

CUT TO:

This is my index finger and that is a door bell, and I will push it now, Ding-Dong, Ding-Dong, and a short pause and Ding-Dong, Ding-Dong.

Through the door's eye, Pavel and I look different now, and not just because of the convexity of the door's eye, but because we've changed our looks entirely.

I'm Vanilla boy and he is Robin the ice.

Nobody shows up so we decide to wait and have a conversation in front of the door.

"Do you know what a Muslim and a Jew would call each other if they were black?" I asked Pavel and he said, "No, I don't. What?"

"You are my brother from another mother." I said and we both laughed low, more like chuckling, and Pavel asked me, "Why is that?"

"Because it's based on the theological books, they are brothers from another mother."

"How come?"

Ding-Dong, Ding-Dong.

"Abraham, had a wife named Sara and a slave woman named Hagar. He couldn't have kids with his wife, so she suggested that Abraham have a son with their slave, Hagar. She became his concubine, and they had a son, Ishmael. Soon after, Sara became pregnant and had a son who they named Isaac, so Sara started some shit with Hagar and Ishmael, and she pushed Abraham to kick them out of their home.

The highest point of irony stands here, God suggested that Abraham listen to Sara. So Abraham kicked out Hagar and his son Ishmael, and the offspring of Ishmael are Muslims while the offspring of Isaac are Jews." I finished the fairytale and, again, Ding-Dong, Ding-Dong.

"So why the fuck do Jews and Muslims try to kill each other?"

In my head came some Self-Soothing and Jelena, and then I said, "I guess Sara understood her mistake when she suggested that Abraham have a son with Hagar and she wanted to correct that, but she couldn't do so by herself, so maybe she left her Will to erase her mistake. If you know what I mean, to kill the sons of Hagar... and

Isaac Newton said for every Action, there is an equal and opposite Reaction."

"So this is why they fight?" asked Pavel and this time he rang the bell; Ding-Dong, Ding-Dong.

"No, they fight because the Jews didn't like their god, so they kicked him off their team. The Muslims took god on their team as a free transfer."

"What about the Christians and Jesus?"

"He's off this season, but he'll come back like the terminator, and no one knows who's team he'll sign up for."

"Yeah, he will resurrect and come back stronger than ever, it's like those reapers when they take off for a few years and then come back with an album that kills everyone." Pavel finished his mediocre joke, and Ding-Dong, Ding-Dong… a short pause, and Pavel asked me, "By the way, how the fuck do you know all of these things about religion? You're an atheist."

I explained to him, that in order to be a doctor you must know the disease.

The door finally opens.

A beautiful lady comes from behind the door and, of course, her Chihuahua is licking her feet.

"Hello, good evening." she said.

"Good evening. Mrs. Prontel. I am doctor Dick Goodpastor and this is my colleague, Doctor Frederick Bah. We are here regarding your mother's prayer. We would like you to invite us inside and talk about your mother's health condition."

Pavel introduced us, and she responded, "Oh yes, sure, please come in."

INT. MRS. PRONTEL'S LIVING ROOM

On our screen comes PAVEL in C.U. he is looking at something, we don't know what he's looking at.

PAVEL moves from our screen and then we see the back of a man, sitting at the dining room table.

We don't see his face or the color of his skin.

In front of him, in the kitchen, we see a beautiful lady cooking.

Now we know that the mystery man is FESTIM, because he was the only one with PAVEL, and the lady is MRS. PRONTEL.

Through the window we can see that it is a very cloudy day, and it's lightly raining.

The camera shoots the dog while it runs on top of the desk and pushes a framed family photo onto the floor. Then, the dog walks toward FESTIM.

From the same angle, like the beginning, the camera shoots FESTIM and MRS. PRONTEL in the kitchen.

FESTIM stretches his hand to reach the knife that lies on the dining room table.

The dog rubs FESTIM's feet with his body and his tail.

FESTIM grabs the dog and puts him on his lap, and starts to caress the dog.

Camera back again at the first angle.

                    MRS. PRONTEL
          Before the storm the silence conquers
          the land, that's what they say. Isn't it
          funny? It's been more than five
          minutes that we haven't said a word.

                    FESTIM
          Yeah…

FESTIM stands up and puts the dog on the table, stabbing him to the death.

MRS. PRONTEL screams.

PAVEL grabs his head with both hands.

His eyes are wide open, as well as his mouth, and he is staring at FESTIM.

FESTIM pulls the gun out from behind him, he points it at MRS. PRONTEL and begins walking toward her.

                    FESTIM
          Shut up bitch, or I'll shoot you.

MRS. PRONTEL zips.

FESTIM grabs her by her hair, pulls her into the living room, and pushes her on the floor.

PAVEL is still wondering, "What the fuck is going on".

                    FESTIM
          PAVEL what the fuck are you looking
          at man? Come on, you're the artist.
          You want some inspiration? Take the
          gun, point it at this bitch and let
          yourself go.

                    PAVEL
          But she didn't do anything.

FESTIM

She didn't do anything? PAVEL,
when I started learning English, the
first thing that I learned was how to
curse, and by coincidence in my
dictionary I found the word bitch. Do
you know what that word means?

PAVEL
(Barely answers)
A bitch, a bitch is a slut, a whore.

FESTIM

No, Pavy. It means a female dog, or
the mother of a dog. So she is a bitch.
She treated her mother like a dog. A
human being wouldn't do that,
because it's against the first instinct of
each animal, and that is the survival
instinct.

PAVEL

But, yes, that's why we call ourselves
humans, that's what we do. We are
predators, parasites, prey,
cocksuckers, weak. Only very few of
us are altruistic, ideologists…

FESTIM

PAVEL, no matter how much we
evolve we cannot escape from that
instinct, otherwise we will be
extinguished and robots or some other
species will rule the world. So PAVEL,
this animal here traded her mother for
a dog. Basically, she is the bitch.

PAVEL

But who cares? This is not my job.

I didn't sign up for this shit.

                    FESTIM
        PAVEL I'm going to fucking shoot
        you, because I don't care either, but, I
        thought that this fucking tragedy
        could inspire you. That you might get
        something out of it.

                    PAVEL
        Well, I don't feel it man! I'm terrified.
        You stabbed the dog and now you
        wanna shoot the lady.

FESTIM points his gun at PAVEL.

                    FESTIM
        Okay, asshole. How about now? Me
        pointing my gun at you, is it inspiring
        or not?

                    PAVEL
        I'm scared. I don't know, I think I'll
        throw up.

                    FESTIM
        Good Pavy, good. Now remember
        those feelings, because you're gonna
        put them on a piece of paper, and
        you're gonna bring them to life.

                    PAVEL
        I don't like horror movies, man!

FESTIM

You ain't no fucking writer, shit. I'm
giving you a chance to experience in
the real world, wrath and violence
that happens every second and you're
just crying like a whore who was just
fucked by a pussy like you.
'I didn't sign up for this, it's not my
job, I didn't sign up for that'. What the
fuck did you sign up for then, Pavy?
To scroll all day on your phone?? You
fucking scroller.

FESTIM (V.O)

The words of my father just came out
of my mouth. Fucking communist me.

PAVEL

I, I, I don't know man, I want to live in
peace.

FESTIM

Yeah peace shit, you piece of shit.
What kind of superhero are you? You
know what, just go and find the trash
bag and put the dog in the trash bag
and clean the fucking table.

PAVEL does exactly as he is told.

FESTIM turns towards MRS.PRONTEL and shoves
his gun in her mouth.

FESTIM

Now you listen, I'm not here to kill
you but I was sent by your mother to
kill your dog and I did

what I was told. So if you wanna call
the cops that is fine, but it will
immediately turn sour for me and I'll
have to shoot you… so the question is,
are we gonna be fine?

MRS. PRONTEL nods her head. And in the moment
when she nodded her head, she nodded more than
she should have which caused FESTIM to pull the
trigger.

Close up of MRS.PRONTEL, her eyes wide open. The
background is bloody red.

PAVEL comes back and sees the Bloody background
and turns his head around so as not to see
MRS.PRONTEL's head blown in half.

              FESTIM
Pavel, I swear to god, I didn't mean to
shoot her. When I asked her to
approve what I said, she nodded too
much and caused me to unwillingly
pull the trigger.

                        CUT TO…

INT. NIGHTCLUB – SAME DAY

PAVEL and FESTIM are having a good time in a
nightclub.

> FESTIM (V.O)
> After what happened today, I need to
> make sure that Pavel has the night of
> his life. I know that, for him, what he
> saw was a living nightmare. After we
> got drunk we went to his home and
> got high.

INT. PAVELS LIVINGROOM – SAME NIGHT

FESTIM and PAVEL are smoking weed and
laughing.

> FESTIM (V.O)
> Pavel got higher than he should have.
> He got so high that he decided to meet
> with god and never come back. It's
> sad because he was young, only
> twenty-something years old. But
> something in my head said: "Yes, die,
> die you fucking Russian spy." And I
> felt so American.
> (Short pause)
> Holy shit.
> I didn't murder the only witness to the
> murder of MRS. PRONTEL.

CUT TO:

Black screen red subtitles

SEASON "Who gives a fuck? We'll keep on going as
long as we are making good money".

EXT.FRONT DOOR – AFTERNOON

DING-DONG, Ding-Dong. No one opened the door, so I decided to go inside anyway, I gently grabbed the door handle and tried to open it. The door wasn't locked so it opened right away. I fished out my gun and slowly walked inside.

And what did I see? A house full of cats, and a douchebag with his headphones on, making a bowl of cheerios. God only knows if he was preparing this bowl himself or for his cats.

Anyway, I pointed my gun at him, and he slowly took off of his headphones and stared at me. I told him how he had become a pussy cat, and how his mother had sent me to kill him. He smiled and said, "Oh, that's right, today is Mother's Day, and thanks to my mother, today I fuck, I roll, and I smoke. I mean, this is insane, she could have aborted me and gone out, had fun, and gotten high. Regardless of what she could have done, I'm thankful for everything she did and didn't do, and, maybe I sound like a psycho and full of shit, but for Mother's Day she deserves flowers. Those flowers are just in case I missed her funeral, so I don't have to go back to the store and tell everyone that my mother died. I feel embarrassed that I think only of that, and then…" and the cat interrupted him. The cat jumped on my hand. I tried to avoid it, and so I unwillingly… well, you know what happened.

What startled me most, however, was what the cats did next. They gathered around the head of this douche, and started licking the blood on the floor. When I saw that, I ran outside, terrified of the cat's behavior.

Zombie cat.
I thought about a superhero move, Super-Zombie-Cat saves the planet from the Rising-Cobra-Clan.

CUT TO:

Black screen, red subtitles.

THE BLACK NAZI

EXT. FRONT OF A DIFFERENT HOUSE

We see FESTIM's finger pressing the doorbell.

DING-DONG.

We see FESTIM at the front door.

In a few seconds the door opens and we see a big black guy.

We don't hear what they are saying to one another.

FESTIM walks inside this house, and the door closes.

INT. BLACK GUY'S HOUSE

FESTIM is looking inside the house and everything looks like a normal house, with nothing special.

> FESTIM (V.O)
> This guy loved his mother, and he didn't trade her for a dog or anything like that, but he was suffering from some kind of spiritual disease and he thought that it would be better if someone else took care of his mother.
> And, just like, that for almost a year no one visited him. So I didn't have any intention to do anything 'unwillingly' to him.

As FESTIM is looking around the room, he sees that in the other room through the open door there is a large picture of a Swastika.

The BLACK GUY is cooking in the kitchen.

>   FESTIM
>   Hey man, are you Nazi? I have never
>   seen black Nazi. (Chuckles)

>   BLACK GUY
>   No I'm not, why?

>   FESTIM
>   You have a big Nazi flag in your
>   room.

BLACK GUY shakes his head, and
chuckles.

>   BLACK GUY
>   That is not Nazi.

>   FESTIM
>   What do you mean, that's not Nazi?

>   BLACK GUY
>   That's the sign of luck, the swastika
>   sign. But since that crazy man used it
>   everyone thinks it's a racist sign.
>   You see isn't it funny? When a great
>   thing falls in the hands of a psycho, it
>   loses any positive value it once had,
>   no matter how enormously significant
>   it was.

>   FESTIM
>   Huh... and I thought I knew
>   everything.

>   BLACK GUY
>   It's seems you don't.

The black guy chops meat with a large knife.

                    BLACK GUY
          It's pathetic to think about the future
          of the white flag. Who knows what it
          will symbolize? How many more
          signs of peace will future children
          come to know as war signs?

                    FESTIM
          Perhaps this is not the best
          comparison, but it's like the word
          FUCK. We can't say it in public
          anymore, even though it's thanks to
          'Fuck' that we humans survive.

The BLACK GUY and FESTIM both chuckle.

                    FESTIM
          Can I walk into that room?

                    BLACK GUY
          Sure, make yourself at home.

FESTIM starts walking slowly toward the room with
the swastika on the wall.

The BLACK GUY follows him from behind, with a
knife in his hand.

Right before FESTIM opens the door to see what's
inside, the BLACK GUY hits FESTIM on the back of
the head with the knife's handle.

FESTIM falls to the floor, unconscious.

                              FADE OUT:

We see two ladies having sex in a very short scene.

White screen

FADE IN:

We turn back to a white screen and slowly our show begins to be seen in color.

INT. BLACK NAZI'S ROOM – SAME DAY

Our screen is still fuzzy. As it gets clearer, we see the BLACK GUY's penis upside down.

This black penis is "small".

Now camera shoots on M.SH. FESTIM

He is hanging upside down and his mouth is taped.

He opens his eyes and when he sees the BLACK GUY naked in front of him, his eyes widen.

Now we have a F.SH. of FESTIM hanging upside down naked, and the BLACK GUY in front of him also naked.

The BLACK GUY has a samurai sword in his hand and his eyes are closed.

FESTIM's penis is "BIG".

PARADOX

Below FESTIM's head is a small tree, about 10 inches tall, a "Bonsai tree".

The whole room is painted white and the walls are divided by red and yellow vertical lines.

In the background we see the picture of the swastika on the wall.

The rope that FESTIM is hanging from is attached to a piece of wood on the high ceiling.

We see one more time the BLACK GUY's penis.

> FESTIM (V.O)
> With my head upside-down and facing him, when I opened my eyes I saw a black dick for the first time, right in front of my face. I have never seen a black dick in my life. I've never seen porn with black people before. I've heard that black men have big dicks, and I was jealous. I envied them. I almost became racist just because of the size of their dicks. Or, to be honest, I was racist… until this moment.
> The size of his dick make me think twice. It enlightened me; and it's not bullshit when they say that in the last moments of your life you'll understand the truth and the meaning of life.

> CUT TO:

INT. DEATH BED

We see a man dying.

> MAN DYING
> I accept that God is for real, and I was his servant.

CUT BACK:

FESTIM (V.O)
Not that. The truth is that all black
people don't have big dicks.

Now I think why the Hollywood guys made that film 'Gentleman
prefer blonde', and gentleman, blonds prefer black, and the sad
truth is that once they go black they never come back. Amy – back
to black. But today, the good news may be, that I have started to
consider that there are possibilities when they go black and back.

The BLACK GUY starts walking in a circle around
FESTIM.

FESTIM(V.O)
This naked person who is circling
around me believed that God
answered his prayers, and that God
sent me to be his sacrifice, and just like
this he must behead me. He'll sprinkle
my blood onto the Bonsai tree and this
will give him heavenly eternal life.

Belief is the result of information that you have regarding a specific
case, and building your life upon the result that you garner from
that information.
Your information could be false or true, and the result will give you
the meaning of your life.
But, if you have false information in your book, then there is
nothing worthy to die for, or to kill for. You must simply run away.

FESTIM starts swinging forward & backward trying
to get lose.

The BLACK GUY begins to move faster around him.

FESTIM keeps moving and shaking like a chicken in
the hands of its master.

After a few laps, the BLACK GUY stops facing
FESTIM.

Our show freezes at this point.

> FESTIM (V.O)
> This abstract picture reminds me of
> Yin & Yang, if you know what I mean.

The BLACK GUY takes the position of a samurai
who is ready to cut God with his sword.

FESTIM moves harder and the rope loosens. FESTIM
falls, his back hitting the Bonsai tree, and it breaks.

The BLACK GUY sees what's just happened.

FESTIM is on the floor trying to untie himself.

Tears fall from the BLACK GUY's eyes.

He sits like a real samurai and does hara-kiri.

FESTIM stops trying to untie himself and just looks
at the BLACK GUY who has just stabbed himself in
the stomach with his samurai sword, committing
suicide. Unwillingly forced by the spiritual world of
his.

> FESTIM (V.O)
> I don't have an opinion about this, but
> one thing came to mind in this
> moment, and that is Yoshimitsu.

CUT TO:

SENTENCE OF THE DAY:

When your motivational speaker is a stupid, racist, bigot, crazy, psychopath, then it's not his fault for resurrecting the racist, bigoted, crazy psychopath animal that's inside you. For starters, you were a racist, bigot, crazy psychopath already, but in the system in which you're living, the sick animal inside of you was sleeping… that is, until your great sick motivational animal came out on stage.

My siblings? Oh yeah, I had a brother and a sister.

Oh, did I mention that I killed my big brother? Unwillingly… that is. I know it's sad, but I have to say that I did it because he… I was protecting myself.

After the rise of communism ended in my country, my older brother was the smartest person in our family, so we voted that he would be in charge of finances. Power moved from my father to him, and I thought that he was better than my father, but, as they say, the apple doesn't fall too far from the tree. He began to act just like my father. For example, you could say anything to him and he would never be insulted. He said that every family member has the right to speak their mind.
Perhaps… but when you're frustrated, violated, persecuted and raped, it's very hard to think before you speak.
However, he kept poisoning our family with fear, telling us that the neighbors hate us, and trying to take everything away from us. I would think about that what he was saying and how he was always keeping us busy with homework and other insignificant mundanities, and anytime I would ask him for money to buy my ticket to go to America and live my dream, he would buy a cake and have a party. Always deceiving us and always keeping us busy. One day I protested against him, and the family became horrified and protected my brother.

I began thinking about ending him. You don't end your big brother in a cliché way. You can't face him with a gun in your hand, that doesn't work, you'll get killed by another family member. You can't talk to anyone about your plan, you can't even think about it yourself.

Time was passing and he was becoming untouchable. I wanted to meet with him; I needed the money for the ticket. I just wanted to ask him one last time to give me the money, and I would be out of his way, but I was his right hand. I was the only one who helped him with his busy work. A good servant like me you wouldn't find ever again.

Like all men in the world, he had only one safe place for self-soothing.

The bathroom.

The bathroom is a synonym for America sometimes. It's the only place where you can contemplate anything, and it's the only place that allows any kind of shit to dwell in it. That's why I sometimes complain about America, because even when you flush that shit down the toilet, it leaves a smell in the air; a smell that makes the bathroom not a very comfortable place for self-soothing, until it fades away.

All it took was an electrical cord. I plugged it in and submerged that cord right into his bath tub.

Hasta la vista, and freedom for all.

Shit, I think I'm losing my mind. I'm not exercising anymore, and I'm having all of these thoughts.

My sister, she loved Leonard DeCaprio. She dreamed of him picking her up in his white Mercedes, taking her back to his place, and licking her pussy. Just like the rest of our family members she used thoughts about movie stars, rock stars, and handsome billionaires for self-soothing.

You can't blame her for feeling this way, but I hated it when she'd tell me how much she loved Leonard DeCaprio, because he's the biggest, smartest racist I've ever seen. I mean, he knows that if we don't stop global warming, one of the things that'll happen is that white people will vanish from the globe. Heat makes people black.

And Leonardo doesn't want that. He's a narcissist. He wants everyone to be like him, white, white, white, like a snowflake, and that will happen if we stop global warming. Everything will become as cold and as white as a snowflake.

Fucking Amor-Alba.

The saddest thing about my sister is that, once, she took a screening test to identify any mental illness she might have had. Maybe she had symptoms that no one ever noticed. Anyway, if they decided that she had an illness, the psychiatrist would take preventive measures.
Of course, like every human, she was diagnosed with Bipolar Depression. The screening test recommended that she see a doctor, and the doctor accepted the diagnoses that the screening test gave her. In order to prevent my sister from doing shit, he prescribed her Shitofuckcockxyn.
 I guess it didn't help her enough, because the next time she saw him, the doctor prescribed her Masmjerrdocalmazin.
The third and last time, she didn't attend her doctor's appointment, because she committed suicide on her 16th birthday.
Although she was now dead, and no longer exists, when she was alive she loved guns. How you can give a gun to a crazy person who suffers from bipolar depression?
We have to come up with a way to stop mass murderers and crazy people from being able to own guns. How do we know who is crazy and to whom we can sell guns?
Well, we have all Americans take a mandatory screening test. Of course, all of them will suffer from Bipolar Depression. And we have to put them all on drugs if they want to buy guns. We all know that guns are for Americans, as being a Superhero is for me. Can't live without my superhero.
Those who don't take the screening test, they suffer from "disobeying the authorities", and we must put them in jail, and maybe we'll give them drugs to free them.

-Lost in American Dream-   Ask your wise hero before you read it.

My grandfather used to put me to sleep by reading fairytales, and I never knew the ending of any of his stories because I'd never stay awake long enough to hear it. Fairytales are made to teach us something, but I was never able to learn anything because I never made it to the end.
I finally began to learn when I started finishing those fairytales.

Jesu's life is funny. Books were meant to teach us something, not to put us to sleep. When you grow up and you read a book that makes you fall asleep, you're either not truly grown up or the book is just boring.

Correction: The sentence that I used earlier JESU'S LIFE IS FUNNY, I meant JESUS, LIFE IS FUNNY.

So let me repeat that last sentence again.
Jesus, life is funny. I never knew what lobotomizing was, but one of my doctor friends showed me how and why they lobotomize people.
A specialist takes a unique needle, and, so as to not penetrate your skull with any kind of drill (which would kill you), with that special needle, they stick you through your eye... well, since we all have the HANDSOME GUY INSURANCE you don't really need to know the 'how', but when they penetrate your eye with the needle, they touch the frontal lobe in your brain and your bodily reaction is to become calm, comfortable and stupidly silent.
For those of you who don't know, let me explain to you that your brain has no pain receptors, so if it were possible for someone to remove your brain without touching your skull, they could take one of those special needles and touch specific spots on your brain and to make you feel however you'd like to. This is not the case, however, and the case is the smartest question ever thought of.
How do you penetrate a person's skull, without causing them suffering? Is there a special gate that might allow us access to the brain without causing pain?
The best answer to this question can be found through examining the effects of television.
All of these years, TV moved freely, invisible as a ninja, and as unstoppable as a virus, inside and outside of my skull, through my

eyes and my ears, lobotomizing me, sedating me, controlling me. How could I have known about this tragedy that was happening inside my head? It was forming its tumor inside of me, and spreading rapidly through my family.

There was no pain.

Who else could lobotomize me?

My father is a communist, my mother is a democrat, and I just wanted to come to America.

No, no, no, Stop.

Don't think like that. Don't even think that if you mix communism and democracy you'll come up with some fresh 'American Dreamer' juice.

I never cared about my parent's ideologies.

I'm simply a product of American TV. Sooner or later, you will see me walking down the street with a price tag on my forehead.

Who else is trying to lobotomize me?

Media, religion, pharma, politics, they sedate me.

What about you? What sedates you? Your life? Your job? Your ugly wife? Your loser husband?

I barely open my eyes.

"This is Sparta" said Leonidas.

I open my eyes and stare at the American flag.

This was my lazy day, so I decided to do nothing, and as an excuse I thought about deaf-mute people. I thought about how they use sign language. You know, every move that I make I have the potential to insult someone, so in order to not offend someone, today I will be like a frozen statue of stacked shit in the center of the world.

"Not good, vanilla boy. In America even if you insult the Pope or fuck the Queen, you have to keep moving, because Jesus won't pay your bills".

Cut off the fingers of the mute-deaf people, and they cannot ask for help.

What about the scrollers? If I cut off their fingers, will they find a way to scroll up and down, left and right, day and night?!

What's wrong with me? I'm so cold and I'm having violent thoughts.

No pulp, no fiction for my life anymore.

CUT TO:

A young Festim and his father.

You know most children never come out of their shell. Instead of helping them hatch and come to life, many parents make their children believe their shells are made of concrete, and, in doing so, they make sure the shell will never crack, and no light will ever pass through.
Few do it for protection, most do it because they are ignorant, and those who do it for protection usually had bad childhood experiences, and a shitty life.
To bring to light the heavenly ideas of the chosen people, that we are saints and they are evil, I have only one thing.
Oh man, kids are fun. They don't recognize languages, cultures, traditions, religions, countries, bullshit, I mean you can teach them anything you want to. For example, one day I taught my nephew to say to my father, in the morning, "Good morning, asshole", and in the evening, "Good evening, piece of shit", and so, every morning and every evening he would say these two phrases to my father.
Is that funny or what?
And, at random moments throughout the day, my nephew would write down and scream Democracy, and would run away from my father. Or, he would tell my mother, "Marilyn sucked my dick", or he would tell my big brother, "You fucking blood-sucker, fuck you", and my nephew would laugh merrily anytime he'd say these things.

It was not god, but me, guiding him on his way to a brighter heavenly future.

And I cry and feel sad when I think about the children of the world, about how many pedophiles are in this world.
Than another question pops into my head, protests, and wants the answer.
If sex is something that makes us happy and comforts us, then are we pedophiles when we feel satisfaction when our kids listen to us and do as we say?

When will we stop treating our children as our property?

"You want to take god from our children!" I heard someone screaming from the crowd.
"Yes, you selfish piece of shit, your children." I responded.
"How about the children? Nooo! I see, it must be your property, because that's what they told you. In order to jack off, you have to make children powerless against you. They will obey you, and make you feel comfortable, like you have superpowers. But guess what? One day, this child will grow up, and you won't be in control anymore. You will be disappointed because you won't have anyone to jack off to anymore so you can feel important, but, bitch, the good news is that you can always adopt or buy a dog.
Even though you are a capitalist and a liberal and blah, blah, blah, you remind me of my father.

To give an end to your story: Ask your doctor, and I bet you 100%, *all* of the money that I get from the sales of this book will be yours if the doctor, the psychiatrist, does not tell you that you suffer from Bipolar Disorder.

DSM Volume V-Five

Everyone is suffering from some sort of disorder and must be put on an expensive drug.

D – Deadly
S – Sucking
M - Money

Fuck you all.

I better go to sleep. Or, did I just wake up from a REM sleep?
Or is this the World War Three?
Yes it is.
This is the end. Am I so useless not to be in the World War Three.
I must be there, this is everything. This is my superhero story. I can't miss that.

I mean think about Achilles fearless. What would happened if he would miss the war, no one would ever remember him.

I already see my name written on the right papyrus pages of hysteria. 'VANILLA BOY a.k.a. flawless, fearless, Braveheart, undisputed and the greatest of all'

World War Three, can't wait to fight in you.

What? You don't want to be a part of the greatest war? You peaceful warrior. What kind of fucking superhero are you?

Superhero who reads books and science shit?

Fuck you.

CUT TO:

INT. LEVIN'S HOUSE

Subtitles on the bottom of the screen

AFTER ONE WEEK

We see that everything is 'normal' in the house.

FESTIM is looking for something in this house.
Slowly, he sneaks into the room that we have not yet seen.

FESTIM slowly opens the door. It's a dark room, and a body wrapping in bandages from head to the toe is lying on the bed.

FESTIM closes the door.

He turns on the flashlight from his phone and fumbles closer to this mummy.

FESTIM wants to unwrap the face of the mummy, but he hears LEVIN and AZOBO talking and walking toward this room.

FESTIM turns off his flashlight and hides inside the closet.

AZOBO and LEVIN walk inside.

Through the closet door we see and hear AZOBO and LEVIN.

> LEVIN
> We have to change the bandage next week, and then she is good for one more month.

> AZOBO
> I can't believe that her son only pays for his mother and never comes to see her or even call her.

> LEVIN
> You don't need to believe it. He paid for a whole year, and it's been four months that she's been dead. Anyway, she has one more month paid for and after that we'll call her son and tell him that we need money for her burial ceremony.

> AZOBO
> What about the other ladies? MONA is getting too fat.

LEVIN

Oh no, no, no. You're giving them too
much food, you have to just give them
enough food to live. If they get skinny
it's because they are old. Nobody will
doubt that you're feeding them. Don't
be fucking ridiculous. You know
you're an immigrant and I'm helping
you, but you have to help me too.

LEVIN and AZOBO walk outside and close the door.

FESTIM slowly opens the closet door, turns the
flashlight on his phone, and unwraps the head of
DEA DISESH.

We see that this old lady has been dead for a long
time.

FESTIM takes out his gun and walks outside, ready
to kill both LEVIN and AZOBO.

LEVIN has already left the house.

AZOBO locks the door and walks toward the
kitchen.

FESTIM walks all the way to the kitchen and points
his gun at AZOBO.

FESTIM
You piece of shit, turn around.

AZOBO turns around, and sees that a gun is pointed
at him.

FESTIM pulls the trigger.

The gun doesn't work.

AZOBO grabs a chair and throws it at FESTIM.

FESTIM ducks and the chair flies over his head.

AZOBO runs inside the mummy's room, and locks the room.

FESTIM chases after AZOBO, but the door is locked.

FESTIM looks around and sees a shotgun hanging on the wall in the living room.

He walks to the shotgun, takes it off of the wall, and looks at it. The shotgun is loaded.

FESTIM turns around and begins to walk slowly toward the mummy's room, calling out to AZOBO.

> FESTIM
> Nurse Reached, come out, come out.
> Nurse Reached. Reached, Reached.

FESTIM points his gun at the door.

> FESTIM
> Nurse Reached, I'm here, ready to
> take you home.

FESTIM shoots a large hole in the door.

Through the hole, the room is dark.

FESTIM slowly walks to the door, puts his head through the hole, looks around inside and calls for AZOBO.

> FESTIM
> Nurse Reached, Jonny is here.

A sharp knife comes toward FESTIM's face.

FESTIM jumps back.

The AZOBO is holding a steak knife, trying to penetrate FESTIM's skull. He comes out through the hole in the door.

We can't say willingly, because FESTIM never planned to harm AZOBO prior to this moment, but we can't say unwillingly either, because AZOBO had committed an inexcusable act right in front of FESTIM.

Perhaps, FESTIM thought about this... perhaps it was just an accident, since FESTIM doesn't stick his nose in someone else's job, and he is busy chasing his American Dream.

FESTIM shoots again at the door, and there is complete silence. AZOBO's hand disappears.

FESTIM takes two steps toward the door and sneaks his head again into the hole in the door.

We have a shot of AZOBO dead, bleeding over the mummy's body.

FESTIM steps back, smiles and looks to his left.

Inside the living room all the ladies are looking at FESTIM, and they Konichiwa him and ask for help.

                    LADIES
            Please, help us too.

                    FESTIM (V.O)
          Well, I just murdered a man. What do
          they mean by saying, "help us too"?

                    LADIES
          PLEASE, we are begging you.

Did I tell you that I'm an expert when it comes to helping people in
need?
My friend Raktim and I were driving on the interstate, and a lot of
stupid people were also on the road. Truck drivers, most of them
are professionals, they don't bullshit on the road, it's true, they piss
in bottles, but they never seem to be in a rush. They take their time,
and holy shit our windshields get dirty. In the history books of
Mosquito civilization, I'm a mass murderer, an expert in
'windshield style'. And for less than a second, I think about the life
of a mosquito. How worthless their lives are, and how many people,
like the slow guy in front of us, deserve to go.
You know, when you are really sick, tired, and old, you are worth
less than a mosquito, and when you are not even good enough for
scientific experiments, I'm not fucking with you, just being honest,
you need to accept the facts. It's your time to do something good if
you have money in the bank, and don't give it to shitty religious
organizations, or the government, or corporations. Give it to science
and go, and if you don't have anything, then just go, and stop being
a burden on the rest of human society.

Whoops, I just killed Gandalf's butterfly and the village of dwarves
are burning in hell.
So, as I was saying, from left to right, Vera, Mona, Rosa, Shelly and
Veronica are laying on their sofa chairs.
This time, it is willingly.
I volunteer, and on their request I prepare the cure for their misery.
I use a water bottle, but there is no water in it. It's my specialty,
mixed juice and some old bacteria, one of the staphylococcus type, a
few drops of sugar, and a few more ingredients, just to make sure
that even the HANDSOME GOOD LOOKING GUY INSURANCE
can't figure out my formula. I have five special needles, and five
special hoes connected to the source of my heavenly cure. I play

Tartini – Devil's Trill Sonata in G minor, and tears fall from my eyes. For the first time in Seattle, the sun shone through the windows and the ladies stepped onto the boat that would lead them to their final and eternal destination, to live forever, happily, after all.

What a great end, I thought

Oh shit, I forgot about Levin.
That motherfucker needs to go too, but I'm thinking I'll get something more out of him, and I'm thinking about making a sequel to this book.

Any suggestions?

You know what, enough with this dream, I'll just tell you in a short way what happened with my carrier and everything else.

CUT TO:

Black screen we see white subtitles in the middle of the screen.

BLASPHEMY ON THE PARAMOUNT OF THE ERECTION

I know this is going to sound radical now, and I'll lose points in heaven's book, but I made my calculations, and, you know, right now I'm in a position that even if I fuck up everything at the end, I'm at so much of an advantage and there's no way for me to lose heaven.

So for all of you 'End' lovers, here is the End.

Keep your complaints, critiques and sarcastic remarks to yourself, because even though I came out of my mother's vagina, I had bigger balls than my father, and right now I'm on my way to becoming what my mother always wanted me to be. Rich, successful, handsome, one of the kind, god himself with a hundred million followers all around the world.

So…

EXT. FRONT YARD OF LEVIN'S HOUSE –
AFTERNOON

LEVIN parks his car in front of his home and runs
inside his house.

INT. LEVIN'S HOUSE

LEVIN opens the front door, walks inside, furiously,
and sees that nobody is there and that everything is
set in its place.

FESTIM is hidden behind the door and from there he
hits LEVIN on the back of his neck.

LEVIN falls to the ground.

FADE OUT:

FADE IN:

INT. LEVIN'S HOUSE – ONE HOUR LATER

We see subtitles on the bottom of the screen.

ONE HOUR LATER

FESTIM is lying on the sofa, drinking coffee.

This insect is evolving in a rapid uncontrollable
revolutionary dragon way.
Franz Kafka would call this book "The Evolution of
the Paradox"

We hear someone is moaning.

FESTIM looks behind him.

                    FESTIM
          Jesus Christ, hallelujah, you finally
          woke up.

Now, our camera in a position where we can see the
stairs, the kitchen and the dining room table, also, in
front of them, in the middle of the screen is the sofa
where FESTIM is having his coffee, and on his black
coffee mug, in pink, BITCH WHERE IS MY COFFEE
is written.

Above FESTIM's head, on the kitchen door LEVIN
has been crucified.

LEVIN starts screaming.

                    FESTIM
          JESUS, shut up, what the hell are you
          screaming for?

                    LEVIN
          You better kill me.

                    FESTIM
          Oh, be patient. Do you remember
          what you said about patience? Things
          will not come to you as you wish, so
          be patient.

                    LEVIN
          You better fucking kill me.

                    FESTIM
Shut the fuck up. Jesus, don't be like
the dead bitch in the Mummy's room,
he was complaining, "just because I'm
black", he ain't even black. He is one
of those lazy shitholes that do nothing
and find excuses for everything that
happens in their life. You know, if you
want something you have to be just
like you, work hard, real hard and, if
it's necessary, you have to fucking
mummify the whole world just to get
what you want.

                    LEVIN
Motherfucker.

FESTIM gets up from the sofa and, holding his
coffee, he turns toward LEVIN.

                    FESTIM
Do I sound like a conservative? Or
better yet, a white racist? I ain't that
either, they fucking cry bad, "Ahhhh,
fucking niggers, Mexicans, we work
and pay taxes, they want to eat for
free, fucking immigrants take our jobs,
ahhhhh". Yeah, fucking immigrants
take your jobs, this is America, there's
no place for crying bitches.

                    LEVIN
        Please, just kill me.

                    FESTIM
        Shut up, Jesus. Let me finish my
        coffee.

Jesus moaning.

FESTIM goes back to sit and continues drinking his
coffee.

                    FESTIM
        Do you know, Jesus, why I'm doing
        this to you? I know in the end you will
        forgive me and we will both go to
        heaven.

                    LEVIN
        You are going to hell.

FESTIM wakes up, but this time he's really angry at
JESUS – LEVIN

                    FESTIM
        What the fuck, Jesus? Why do only I
        go to hell? You promised everyone
        heaven. This is injustice. Just because
        I'm an atheist. I know my human
        rights. You know what, Jesus? For the
        first time in my life I'm begging you
        for one thing, please go back on your
        word.

                    JESUS
        You are gonna die like piece of shit.

                         FESTIM
          You are making a big fucking mistake,
          Jesus, and this is not the first time. I
          hate the fact that when I was young I
          wasn't big enough to stop you from
          slaying my brothers and sisters. For
          the first time in my life, I saw the
          wrath that you unleashed upon my
          family, and I was only three years old.
          Jesus, this is your end, say your last
          words before I blow your fucking
          head off.

                         JESUS
          FUCK YOU ALL.

And again unwillingly, forced by an evil
environment and the great ambition for a better
future, FESTIM is a victim of a crazy, selfish, unfair,
ugly society and pulls the trigger until there are no
more bullets in his gun. Bang, bang, bang, bang,
bang, bang, bang, click, click, click…

Jesus is dead.

                         FESTIM
          I've killed JESUS, and I'm not even a
          Jew.
          Ich bin Ubermensch.

FESTIM goes into the kitchen, pours some more
coffee, and comes back to sit on the sofa.

Slowly from the F.SH. of the entire set, we zoom into
FESTIM's face until we have a close up of FESTIM.
The music playing in the background is MOZART –
REQUIEM.

How far we have come?
Our lives became business. Our ideals we leave as a bait in the bank trying to cash out our souls.
While the children are taken hostage from the corporate and growing up as slaves.

Word of the day: DREAM

The sentence and the lesson of the day: The German word for Dream is Traum, and in the Greek language Traum means Trauma.

So, does this mean that all my life I wished to live the American Trauma?

Another synonym for Trauma, is Nightmare.

Is this why our lives are so disgusting, frightening, terrible, ugly, and miserable?
Is this why anytime I have a genius idea that will make everyone happy, everyone says that it would be great, but it can happen only in dreams? Is it because they have been lobotomized in a way that makes them believe that good things can't happen in reality, only in dreams?
Is this why anytime we are having a bad dream, we hope it is just a dream and not reality? Is it because we were told that only reality can be evil and cruel, and that Trauma is actually a good thing?
Let's think positive. Everything that I said about the word dream above doesn't mean shit. Dreams are the only place beyond the rainbow where our wishes can come true.
I lived the American Dream, I fucked, I danced, I got money, I drove expensive cars, I did drugs, I became rich, I bought a yacht, I owned guns, I conquered, I slaved, I killed, I cheated, I this and I that.

But what if positivity doesn't work, and the place beyond the rainbow has turned into a nightmare? Your home has become the hell. Then where do you go, little, white, freckle-faced Dorothy?
I'm not sure if we can make your dream white again…

I walked through the backyard of Jesus's house, and the beautiful green grass in the yard reminded me of home. So I walked on that grass, and when I took my third step I stepped in dog shit. I had to be careful, because American grass is full of dog shit, I mean civilized grass.

That shit brought me back to reality, and I thought, "Why is there always some piece of shit that has to bring me back to reality?" And then I didn't do anything. I didn't even take my foot off of the shit. I just looked at the clouds, spread out in the sky, and I tried to give their shapes meaning.

This time I found myself on my right papyrus page, I told myself that from now on, I would be a better person. I will never think twice to help those in need. I will never try to take advantage of anyone. I will study every single day. I will become like a black hole, traveling and flying through the greatness of space, and I will suck knowledge like a black hole would suck in stars and entire galaxies. I will be thankful to all of the people in the world, and I will ask for forgiveness from nature.

I will love unconditionally, and I will set myself free.

Suddenly I'm naked and I open my arms. In my left hand, I'm holding that black coffee mug with pink letter spelling out, *WHERE IS MY COFFEE BITCH,* and in my right hand I hold the empty gun, and I don't know if I'm flying, or if the world is falling.

I look down on the face of the earth for one last time and the world looks so small, and it was becoming smaller and smaller, and for the last time I wanted to come on the face of the earth, but my hands were busy. I thought about Marilyn and even that didn't help. I wanted so badly to do that elevating, self-soothing action for the last time, so I let my empty gun go, falling down to earth and…

"It's not about freedom. It's about being free to find something that you love and letting yourself loose in it, until eternity carves your name into the papyrus, lost forever, happily, and never found page."

Nature

Life fucked us all, but you don't have to be its bitch.

Printed in Great Britain
by Amazon